Rabindranath Tagore - Broken Ties and Other Stories

Rabindranath Tagore (1861-1941) who was a gifted Bengali Renaissance man, distinguishing himself as a philosopher, social and political reformer and a popular author in all literary genres. He was instrumental in an increased freedom for the press and influenced Gandhi and the founders of modern India.

He composed hundreds of songs which are still sung today as they include the Indian and Bangladesh's national anthems.

His prolific literary life has left a legacy of quality novels, essays and in this volume his shorter works.

Together his works earned him the distinction of being the first Asian writer to receive the Nobel Prize in Literature in 1913.

INDEX OF CONTENTS

BROKEN TIES

CHAPTER I

UNCLE

I

When I first met Satish he appeared to me like a constellation of stars, his eyes shining, his tapering fingers like flames of fire, his face glowing with a youthful radiance. I was surprised to find that most of his fellow-students hated him, for no other fault than that he resembled himself more than he resembled others. Because with men, as well as with some insects, taking the colour of the surroundings is often the best means of self-protection.

The students in the hostel where I lived could easily guess my reverence for Satish. This caused them discomfort, and they never missed an opportunity of reviling him in my hearing. If you have a speck of grit in your eye it is best not to rub it. And when words smart it is best to leave them unanswered.

But one day the calumny against Satish was so gross that I could not remain silent.

Yet the trouble was that I hardly knew anything about Satish. We never had even a word between us, while some of the other students were his close neighbours, and some his distant relatives. These affirmed, with assurance, that what they said was true; and I affirmed, with even greater assurance, that it was incredible. Then all the residents of the hostel bared their arms, and cried: 'What impertinence!'

That night I was vexed to tears. Next day, in an interval between lectures, when Satish was reading a book lying at full length on the grass in College Square, I went up to him without any introduction, and spoke to him in a confused manner, scarcely knowing what I said. Satish shut his book, and looked in my face. Those who have not seen his eyes will not know what that look was like.

Satish said to me: 'Those who libel me do so, not because they love to know the truth, but because they love to believe evil of me. Therefore it is useless to try to prove to them that the calumny is untrue.'

'But,' I said,'the liars must be -'

'They are not liars,' interrupted Satish.

'I have a neighbour,' he went on, 'who has epileptic fits. Last winter I gave him a blanket. My servant came to me in a furious temper, and told me that the boy only feigned the disease. These students who malign me are like that servant of mine. They believe what they say. Possibly my fate has awarded me an extra blanket which they think would have suited them better.'

I asked him a question: 'Is it true what they say, that you are an atheist?'

He said: 'Yes.'

I bent my head to the ground. I had been arguing with my fellow-students that Satish could not possibly be an atheist.

I had received two severe blows at the outset of my short acquaintance with Satish. I had imagined that he was a Brahman, but I had come to know that Satish belonged to a Bania family, and I in whose veins flowed a bluer blood was bound duly to despise all Banias. Secondly, I had a rooted belief that atheists were worse than murderers, nay, worse even than beef-eaters.

Nobody could have imagined, even in a dream, that I would ever sit down and take my meals with a Bania student, or that my fanatical zeal in the creed of atheism would surpass even that of my instructor. Yet both these things came to pass.

Wilkins was our professor in the College. His learning was on a level with his contempt for his pupils. He felt that it was a menial occupation to teach literature to Bengali students. Therefore, in our Shakespeare class, he would give us the synonym for 'cat' as 'a quadruped of the feline species.' But Satish was excused from taking notes. The Professor told him: 'I will make good to you the hours wasted in this class when you come to my room.'

The other less favoured students used to ascribe this indulgent treatment of Satish to his fair complexion and to his profession of atheism. Some of the more worldly-wise among them went to

Wilkins's study with a great show of enthusiasm to borrow from him some book on Positivism. But he refused, saying that it would be too hard for them. That they should be held unfit even to cultivate atheism made their minds all the more bitter against Satish.

II

Jagamohan was Satish's uncle. He was a notorious atheist of that time. It would be inadequate to say that he did not believe in God. One ought rather to say that he vehemently believed in no God. As the business of a captain in the navy is rather to sink ships than to steer, so it was Jagamohan's business to sink the creed of theism, wherever it put its head above the water.

The order of his arguments ran like this:

(1) If there be a God, then we must owe our intelligence to Him.

(2) But our intelligence clearly tells us that there is no God.

(3) Therefore God Himself tells us that there is no God.

'Yet you Hindus,' he would continue, 'have the effrontery to say that God exists. For this sin thirty-three million gods and goddesses exact penalties from you people, pulling your ears hard for your disobedience.'

Jagamohan was married when he was a mere boy. Before his wife died he had read Malthus. He never married again.

His younger brother, Harimohan, was the father of Satish. Harimohan's nature was so exactly the opposite of his elder brother's, that people might suspect me of fabricating it for the purpose of writing a story. But only stories have to be always on their guard to sustain their reader's confidence. Facts have no such responsibility, and laugh at our incredulity. So, in this world, there are abundant instances of two brothers, the exact opposites of one another, like morning and evening.

Harimohan, in his infancy, had been a weakly child. His parents had tried to keep him safe from the attacks of all maladies by barricading him behind amulets and charms, dust taken from holy shrines, and blessings bought from innumerable Brahmans at enormous expense. When Harimohan grew up, he was physically quite robust, yet the tradition of his poor health lingered on in the family. So nobody claimed from him anything more arduous than that he should continue to live. He fulfilled his part, and did hold on to his life. Yet he never allowed his family to forget for a moment that life in his case was more fragile than in most other mortals. Thus he managed to divert towards himself the undivided attention of all his aunts and his mother, and had specially prepared meals served to him. He had less work and more rest than other members of the family. He was never allowed to forget that he was under the special protection, not only of his aforesaid mother and aunts, but also of the countless gods and goddesses presiding in the three regions of earth, heaven, and air. He thus acquired an attitude of prayerful dependence towards all the powers of the world, both seen and unseen, sub-inspectors, wealthy neighbours, highly placed officials, let alone sacred cows and Brahmans.

Jagamohan's anxieties went altogether in an opposite direction. He would give a wide berth to men of power, lest the slightest suspicion of snobbishness should cling to him. It was this same sentiment which had greatly to do with his defiance of the gods. His knees were too stiff to bend before those from whom favour could be expected.

Harimohan got himself married at the proper time, that is to say, long before the time. After three sisters and three brothers, Satish was born. Everybody was struck by his resemblance to his uncle, and Jagamohan took possession of him, as if he were his own son.

At first Harimohan was glad of this, having regard to the educational advantage of the arrangement; for Jagamohan had the reputation of being the most eminent scholar of that period.

He seemed to live within the shell of his English books. It was easy to find the rooms he occupied in the house by the rows of books about the walls, just as it is easy to find out the bed of a stream by its lines of pebbles.

Harimohan petted and spoilt his eldest son, Purandar, to his heart's content. He had an impression that Purandar was too delicate to survive the shock of being denied anything he wanted. His education was neglected. No time was lost in getting him married, and yet nobody could keep him within the connubial limits. If Harimohan's daughter-in-law expressed any disapprobation of his vagaries in that direction,

Harimohan would get angry with her and ascribe his son's conduct to her want of tact and charm.

Jagamohan entirely took charge of Satish to save him from similar paternal solicitude. Satish acquired a mastery of the English language while he was still a child, and the inflammatory doctrines of Mill and Bentham set his brain on fire, till he began to burn like a living torch of atheism.

Jagamohan treated Satish, not as his junior, but as his boon companion. He held the opinion that veneration in human nature was a superstition, specially designed to make men into slaves. Some son-in-law of the family wrote to him a letter, with the usual formal beginning:

'To the gracious feet of -'

Jagamohan wrote an answer, arguing with him as follows:

MY DEAR NOREN Neither you nor I know what special significance it gives to the feet to call them 'gracious.' Therefore the epithet is worse than useless, and had better be dropped. And then it is apt to give one a nervous shock when you address your letter only to the feet, completely ignoring their owner. But you should understand, that so long as my feet are attached to my body, you should never dissociate them from their context.

Next, you should bear in mind that human feet have not the advantage of prehensibility, and it is sheer madness to offer anything to them, confounding their natural function.

Lastly, your use of the plural inflection to the word 'feet,' instead of the dual, may denote special reverence on your part (because there are animals with four feet which have your particular veneration) but I consider it my duty to disabuse your mind of all errors concerning my own zoological identity. Yours, JAGAMOHAN.

Jagamohan used to discuss with Satish subjects which are usually kept out of sight in conversation. If people objected to this plainness of speech with one so young, he would say that you can only drive away hornets by breaking in their nest. So you can only drive away the shamefulness of certain subjects by piercing through the shame itself.

When Satish had completed his College course, Harimohan tried his best to extricate him from his uncle's sphere of influence. But when once the noose is fixed round the neck, it only grows tighter by pulling at it. Harimohan became more and more annoyed at his brother, the more Satish proved recalcitrant. If this atheism of his son and elder brother had been merely a matter of private opinion, Harimohan could have tolerated it. He was quite ready to pass off dishes of fowl as 'kid curry.' [Footnote: In Bengal kid curry is often eaten without blame. But fowl curry would come within the prohibitions.] But matters had now become so desperate that even lies became powerless to whitewash the culprits. What brought things to a head was this:

The positive side of Jagamohan's atheistic creed consisted in doing good to others. He felt a special pride in it, because doing good, for an atheist, was a matter of unmitigated loss. It had no allurements of merit and no deterrents of punishment in the hereafter. If he was asked what concern he had in bringing about'the greatest happiness of the greatest number,' he used to answer that his best incentive was that he could expect nothing in return. He would say to Satish:

'Baba, [Footnote: A term of endearment, literally 'father.'] we are atheists. And therefore the very pride of it should keep us absolutely stainless. Because we have no respect for any being higher than ourselves, therefore we must respect ourselves.'

There were some leather shops in the neighbourhood kept by Muhammadans. The uncle and nephew bestirred themselves with great zeal in doing good to these Muhammadans and their untouchable leather workers! [Footnote: As leather is made from the hides of dead animals, those who work in leather are regarded as unclean by orthodox Hindus. Only the very lowest castes are tanners.] This made Harimohan beside himself with indignation. Since he knew that any appeal to Scriptures, or to tradition, would have no effect upon these two renegades, he complained to his brother concerning the wasting of his patrimony.

'When my expenditure,' his brother answered, 'comes up to the amount you have spent upon your full-fed Brahman priests, we shall be quits.'

One day Harimohan's people were surprised to find that a preparation was going on in Jaga-mohan's quarters for a grand feast. The cooks and waiters were all Mussulmans. Harimohan called for his son, and said to him angrily:

'I hear that you are going to give a feast to all your reverend friends, the leather workers.'

Satish replied that he was far too poor to think of it. His uncle had invited them. Purandar, Satish's elder brother, was equally indignant. He threatened to drive all the unclean guests away. When Harimohan expressed his protest to his brother, he answered:

'I never make any objection to your offering food to your idols. You should make no objection to my offering food to my gods.'

'Your gods!' exclaimed Harimohan.

'Yes, my gods,' his brother answered.

'Have you become a theist all of a sudden?' sneered Harimohan.

'No!' his brother replied. 'Theists worship the God who is invisible. You idolaters worship gods who are visible, but dumb and deaf. The gods I worship are both visible and audible, and it is impossible not to believe in them.'

'Do you really mean to say,' cried Harimohan, 'that these leather workers and Mussulmans are your gods?'

'Indeed, they are,' said Jagamohan; 'you shall see their miraculous power when I put food before them. They will actually swallow it, which I defy your gods to do. It delights my heart to see my gods perform such divine wonders. If you are not morally blind, it will delight your heart also.'

Purandar came to his uncle, and told him in a high-pitched voice that he was prepared to take desperate measures to stop the proceedings. Jagamohan laughed at him, and said:

'You monkey! If you ever try to lay hands on my gods, you will instantly discover how powerful they are, and I shall not have to do anything to defend them.'

Purandar was even a greater coward than his father. He was a tyrant only where he was sure of receiving submission. In this case he did not dare to pick a quarrel with his Muhammadan neighbours. So he came to Satish, and reviled him. Satish gazed at him with those wonderful eyes of his, and remained silent.

The feast was a great success.

III

Harimohan could not take this insult passively. He declared war. The property on whose income the whole family subsisted was a temple endowment. Harimohan brought a suit in the law court against his brother, accusing him of such grave breaches of propriety as made him unworthy of remaining the trustee of a religious endowment. Harimohan had as many witnesses as ever he wished. The whole Hindu neighbourhood was ready to support him.

Jagamohan professed in open court that he had no faith in gods or idols of any description whatever; that all eatable food was for him food to be eaten; that he never bothered his head to find out the particular limb of Brahma from which the Muhammadans had issued, and therefore he had not the smallest hesitation in taking food in their company.

The judge ruled Jagamohan to be unfit to hold the temple property. Jagamohan's lawyers assured him that the decision could be upset by an appeal to the higher Court. But Jagamohan refused to appeal. He said he could not cheat even the gods whom he did not believe in. Only those who had the intelligence to believe such things had the conscience to cheat them.

His friends asked him: 'How are you going to maintain yourself?'

He answered: 'If I have nothing else to eat, I shall be content to gulp down my last breath.'

After this, a partition was made of the family house. A wall was raised from the ground floor to the upper storey, dividing the house into two parts.

Harimohan had great faith in the selfish sanity of prudence in human nature. He was certain that the savour of good living would tempt Satish into his golden trap, away from the empty nest of Jagamohan. But Satish gave another proof that he had neither inherited his father's conscience nor his sanity. He remained with his uncle.

Jagamohan was so accustomed to look upon Satish as his own that he was not surprised to find him remaining on his side after the partition.

But Harimohan knew his brother's temperament very well. He went about talking to people, explaining that the reason why Jagamohan did not let go his hold on Satish was that he expected to make a good thing out of Satish's presence, keeping him as a kind of hostage.

Harimohan almost shed tears while he said to his neighbour: 'Could my brother ever imagine that I was going to starve him? Since he is cunning enough to concoct this diabolical plot against me, I shall wait and see whether he is cleverer than I am.'

Harimohan's talk about Satish reached Jaga-mohan's ears. Jagamohan was surprised at his own stupidity in not anticipating such a turn of events.

He said: 'Good-bye, Satish.'

Satish was absolutely certain that nothing could make Jagamohan change his mind, so he had to take his leave, after having spent his eighteen years of life in his uncle's company.

When Satish had put his books and bedding on the top of the carriage, and driven away, Jagamohan shut the door of his room, and flung himself on the floor. When evening came, and the old servant knocked at the door with the lighted lamp, he got no answer.

Alas for the greatest happiness of the greatest number! The estimate in number is not the only measure of human affairs. The man who counts 'one' may go beyond all arithmetic when the heart does the sum. When Satish took his departure, he at once became infinite to Jagamohan.

Satish went into a students' lodging to share a room with one of his friends. Harimohan shed tears while meditating on the neglect of filial duties in this god-forsaken age. Harimohan had a very tender heart.

After the partition, Purandar dedicated a room in their portion of the house to the family god. It gave him a peculiar pleasure to know that his uncle must be execrating him for the noise raised every morning and every evening by the sacred conches and prayer gongs.

In order to maintain himself, Satish secured a post as a private tutor. Jagamohan obtained an appointment as head master of a high school. And it became a religious duty with Harimohan and Purandar to persuade parents and guardians to take away their boys from the malign influence of the atheist Jagamohan.

IV

One day, after a very long interval of absence, Satish came to Jagamohan. These two had given up the usual form of greeting [Footnote: This greeting in Bengal is for the younger to touch the feet of the elder.] which passes between elder and younger.

Jagamohan embraced Satish, led him to a chair, and asked him for the news.

There was news indeed!

A girl named Nonibala had taken shelter with her widowed mother in the house of the mother's brother. So long as her mother lived, there was no trouble. But a short time ago her mother had died. Her cousins were rascals. One of their friends had taken away this girl. Then, suspecting her of infidelity, after a while he made her life a constant torture. This had happened in the house next to the one where Satish had his tutorship. Satish wanted to save her from this misery, but he had no money or shelter of his own. Therefore he had come to his uncle. The girl was about to give birth to a child.

Jagamohan, when he heard the story, was filled with indignation. He was not the man to calculate coldly the consequence of his deeds, and he at once said to his nephew: 'I have the room in which I keep my books. I can put the girl there.'

'But what about your books?' Satish asked in surprise. Very few books, however, were now remaining. During the time when he had been unable to secure an appointment, he had been obliged to eke out a living by selling his books.

Jagamohan said: 'Bring the girl at once.'

'She is waiting downstairs,' said Satish. 'I have brought her here.' Jagamohan ran downstairs, and found the girl crouching in the corner, wrapped in her sari, looking like a bundle of clothes.

Jagamohan, in his deep bass voice, said at once: 'Come, little Mother, why do you sit in the dust?'

The girl covered her face, and burst into tears. Jagamohan was not a man to give way to emotion, but his eyes were wet as he turned to Satish and said: 'The burden that this girl is bearing is ours.'

Then he said to the girl: 'Mother, don't be shy on my account. My schoolfellows used to call me "Mad Jagai," and I am the same madcap even now.'

Then, without hesitation, he took the girl by both her hands, and raised her. The veil dropped from off her face.

The girl's face was fresh and young, and there was no line of hardness or vice in it. The inner purity of her heart had not been stained, just as a speck of dust does not soil a flower. Jagamohan took Nonibala to his upper room, and said to her: 'Mother, look what a state my room is in! The floor is all unswept. Everything is upside down; and as for myself, I have no fixed hour for my bath or my meals. Now that you have come to my house, everything will be put right, and even this mad Jagai will be made respectable.'

Nonibala had never felt before, even when her mother lived, how much one person could be to another; because her mother had looked upon her, not so much as a daughter, but as a young girl who had to be watched.

Jagamohan employed an elderly woman servant to help Nonibala. At first Noni was afraid lest Jagamohan should refuse to take food from her hand because of her impurity. But it turned out that Jagamohan refused to take his meals unless they were cooked and served by Noni.

Jagamohan was aware that a great wave of calumny was about to break over his head. Noni also felt that it was inevitable, and she had no peace of mind. Within a day or two it began.

The servant who waited on her had at first supposed that Noni was Jagamohan's daughter. But she came one day, saying hard things to Noni, and resigned her service in contempt. Noni became pale with fear, thinking of Jagamohan.

Jagamohan said to her: 'My little Mother, the full moon is up in the horizon of mr life, so the time is ripe for the flood-tide of revilement. But, however muddy the water may become, it will never stain my moonlight.'

An aunt of Jagamohan's came to Harimohan's quarters, and said to him: 'Jagai, what a disgrace, what a disgrace! Wipe off this stain of sin from your house.'

Jagamohan answered: 'You are pious people, and this advice is worthy of you. But if I try to drive away all relics of sin, what will become of the sinner?'

Some old grandmother of a woman came to him, and said: 'Send this wench away to the hospital. Harimohan is ready to bear all the cost.'

Jagamohan said: 'But she is my mother. Because some one is ready to pay expenses, should I send my mother to the hospital?'

The grandmother opened her eyes wide with surprise and said: 'Who is this you call your mother?'

Jagamohan replied: 'Her who nourished life within her womb, and risks her life to give birth to children. I cannot call that scoundrel-father of the child "Father." He can only cause trouble, keeping himself safely out of it.'

Harimohan's whole body shrank with the utter infamy of the thing. That a fallen woman should be sheltered only on the other side of the wall, and in the midst of a household sacred to the memory of generations of mothers and grandmothers! The disgrace was intolerable.

Harimohan at once surmised that Satish was mixed up in this affair, and that his uncle was encouraging him in his shameful conduct. He was so sure of his facts that he went about spreading the news. Jagamohan did not say a single word to contradict him.

'For us atheists,' he said,'the only heaven waiting for good deeds is calumny.'

The more the rumour of Jagamohan's doings became distorted, the more he seemed to enjoy it, and his laughter rang loud in the sky. Harimohan and respectable people of his class could never imagine that the uncle could go so far as to jest openly on such a subject, and indulge in loud unseemly buffoonery about it with his own nephew.

Though Purandar had been carefully avoiding that part of the house where his uncle lived, he vowed that he would never rest till he had driven the girl away from her shelter.

At the time when Jagamohan had to go to his school he would shut up all access to his quarters, and he would come back the moment he had any leisure to see how Noni was faring.

One day at noon Purandar, with the help of a bamboo ladder, crossed the boundary wall and jumped down into Jagamohan's part of the house. Nonibala had been resting after the morning meal. The door of her room was open. Purandar, when he saw the sleeping figure of Noni, gave a great start, and shouted out in anger: 'So you are here, are you?'

Noni woke up and saw Purandar before her. She became pale as death, and her limbs shrank under her. She felt powerless to run away or to utter a single word.

Purandar, trembling with rage, shouted out: 'Noni!'

Just then Jagamohan entered the room from behind, and cried: 'Get out of this room.'

Purandar's whole body began to swell up like an angry cat.

Jagamohan said: 'If you don't get out at once, I will call in the police.'

Purandar darted a terrible glance at Noni, and went out. Noni fainted.

Jagamohan now understood the whole situation. By questioning, he found out that Satish had been aware that Purandar had seduced Noni; but, fearing an angry brawl, he had not informed Jagamohan of the fact.

For days after this incident Noni trembled like a bamboo leaf. Then she gave birth to a dead child.

One midnight Purandar had driven Noni away from her room, kicking her in anger. Since then he had sought her in vain. When he suddenly found her in his uncle's house, he was seized with an uncontrollable passion of jealousy. He was sure that Satish had enticed her away from him, to keep her for his own pleasure, and had then put her in the very next house to his own in order to insult him. This was more than any mortal man could bear.

Harimohan heard all about it. Indeed, Purandar never took any pains to hide these doings from his father, for his father looked upon his son's moral aberrations with a kindly indulgence. But Harimohan thought it contrary to all notions of decency for Satish to snatch away this girl whom his elder brother, Purandar, had looked upon with favour. He devoutly hoped that Purandar would be successful in recovering his spoil.

It was the time of the Christmas holidays. Jagamohan attended Noni night and day. One evening he was translating a novel of Sir Walter Scott's to her, when Purandar burst into the room with another young man.

When Jagamohan was about to call for the police, the young man said: 'I am Noni's cousin. I have come to take her away.'

Jagamohan caught hold of Purandar by his neck, and shoved him out of the room and down the stairs. He then turned to the other young man and said: 'You are a villain and a scoundrel! You assert this cousin's right of yours to wreck her life, not to protect her.'

The young man hurried away. But when he had got to a safe distance, he threatened Jagamohan with legal steps in order to rescue his ward.

Noni said within herself: 'O Earth, open and swallow me up!' [Footnote: The reference is to Sita in the Ramayana, who uttered this cry when in extreme trouble.]

Jagamohan called Satish, and said to him: 'Let me leave this place and go to some up-country town with Noni. It will kill her if this is repeated.'

Satish urged that his brother was certain to follow her when once he had got the clue.

'Then what do you propose?' said Jagamohan.

'Let me marry Noni,' was the answer.

'Marry Noni!'

'Yes, according to the civil marriage rites.'

Jagamohan stood up and went to Satish, and pressed him to his heart.

Since the partition of the house, Harimohan had not once entered the house to see his elder brother. But that day he came in, dishevelled, and said:

'Dada, [Footnote: Elder brother.] what disaster is this you are planning?'

'I am saving everybody from disaster,' said Jagamohan.

'Satish is just like a son to you,' said Harimohan, 'and yet you can have the heart to see him married to that woman of the street!'

'Yes,' he replied, 'I have brought him up almost as my own son, and I consider that my pains have borne fruit at last.'

'Dada,' said Harimohan, 'I humbly acknowledge my defeat at your hands. I am willing to write away half my property to you, if only you will not take revenge on me like this.'

Jagamohan started up from his chair and bellowed out:

'You want to throw me your dirty leavings, as you throw a dog a bone! I am an atheist, remember that! I am not a pious man like you! I neither take revenge, nor beg for favours.'

Harimohan hastened round to Satish's lodgings. He cried out to him:

'Satish! What in the world are you going to do? Can you think of no other way of ruining yourself? Are you determined to plunge the whole family into this hideous shame?'

Satish answered: 'I have no particular desire to marry. I only do it in order to save my family from hideous shame.'

Harimohan shouted: 'Have you not got the least spark of conscience left in you? That girl, who is almost like a wife to your brother'

Satish caught him up sharply: 'What? Like a wife. Not that word, sir, if you please!'

After that, Harimohan became wildly abusive in his language, and Satish remained silent.

What troubled Harimohan most was that Purandar openly advertised his intention to commit suicide if Satish married Noni. Purandar's wife told him that this would solve a difficult problem, if only he would have the courage to do it.

Satish sedulously avoided Noni all these days, but, when the proposed marriage was settled, Jagamohan asked Satish that Noni and he should try to know each other better before they were united in wedlock. Satish consented.

Jagamohan fixed a date for their first talk together. He said to Noni:

'My little Mother, you must dress yourself up for this occasion.'

Noni bent her eyes to the ground.

'No, no,' said he,'don't be shy, Noni. I have a great longing to see you nicely dressed, and you must satisfy my desire.'

He had specially selected some Benares silk and a bodice and veil for Noni. He gave these things to her.

Noni prostrated herself at his feet. This made Jagamohan get up hurriedly. He snatched away his feet from her embrace, and said:

'I see, Noni, I have miserably failed in clearing your mind of all this superstitious reverence. I may be your elder in age, but don't you know you are greater than I am, for you are my mother?'

He kissed her on her forehead and said:

'I have had an invitation to go out, and I shall be late back this evening.'

Noni clasped his hand and said:

'Baba, I want your blessing to-night.'

Jagamohan replied:

'Mother, I see that you are determined to turn me into a theist in my old age. I wouldn't give a brass farthing for a blessing, myself. Yet I cannot help blessing you when I see your face.'

Jagamohan put his hand under her chin, and raised her face, and looked into it silently, while tears ran down her cheeks.

In the evening a man ran up to the place where Jagamohan was having his dinner, and brought him back to his house.

He found the dead body of Noni, stretched on the bed, dressed in the things he had given her. In her hand was a letter. Satish was standing by her head. Jagamohan opened the letter, and read:

Baba, forgive me. I could not do what you wanted. I tried my best, but I could never forget him. My thousand salutations to your gracious feet. NONIBALA, the Sinner.

CHAPTER II

SATISH

I

The last words of Jagamohan, the atheist, to his nephew, Satish, were: 'If you have a fancy for funeral ceremony, don't waste it on your uncle, reserve it for your father.'

This is how he came by his death.

When the plague first broke out in Calcutta, the poor citizens were less afraid of the epidemic than of the preventive staff who wore its badge. Satish's father, Harimohan, was sure that their Mussulman neighbours, the untouchable leather-dealers, would be the first to catch it, and thereupon defile him and his kith and kin by dragging them along into a common end. Before he fled from his house, Harimohan went over to offer refuge to his elder brother, saying: 'I have taken a house on the river at Kalna, if you -'

'Nonsense!' interrupted Jagamohan. 'How can I desert these people?'

'Which people?'

'These leather-dealers of ours.'

Harimohan made a grimace and left his brother without further parley. He next proceeded to his son's lodgings, and to him simply said: 'Come along.'

Satish's refusal was equally laconic. 'I have work to do here,' he replied.

'As pall-bearer to the leather-dealers, I suppose?'

'Yes, sir; that is, if my services be needed.'

'Yes, sir, indeed! You scamp, you scoundrel, you atheist! If need be you're quite ready to consign fourteen generations of your ancestors to perdition, I have no doubt!'

Convinced that the Kali Yuga [Footnote: According to the Hindu Shastras the present age, the Kali Yuga, is the Dark Age when Dharma (civilisation) will be at its lowest ebb.] had touched its lowest depth, Harimohan returned home, despairing of the salvation of his next of kin. In order to protect himself against contamination he covered sheets of foolscap with the name of Kali, the protecting goddess, in his neatest handwriting.

Harimohan left Calcutta. The plague and the preventive officials duly made their appearance in the locality; and for dread of being dragged off to the plague hospital, the wretched victims dared not call in medical aid. After a visit to one of these hospitals, Jagamohan shook his head and remarked: 'What if these people are falling ill, that does not make them criminals.'

Jagamohan schemed and contrived till he obtained permission to use his own house as a private plague hospital. Some of us students offered to assist Satish in nursing: there was a qualified doctor among our number.

The first patient in our hospital was a Mussulman. He died. The next was Jagamohan himself. He did not survive either. He said to Satish:

'The religion I have all along followed has given me its last reward. There is nothing to complain of.'

Satish had never taken the dust [Footnote: Touching the feet of a revered elder, and then one's own head, is called taking the dust of the feet. It is the formal way of doing reverence.] of his uncle's feet while living. After Jagamohan's death he made that obeisance for the first and last time.

'Fit death for an atheist!' scoffed Hari-mohan when he first came across Satish after the cremation.

'That is so, sir!' agreed Satish, proudly.

II

Just as, when the flame is blown out, the light suddenly and completely disappears, so did Satish after his uncle's death. He went out of our ken altogether.

We had never been able to fathom how deeply Satish loved his uncle. Jagamohan was alike father and friend to him, and, it may be said, son as well; for the old man had been so regardless of himself, so unmindful of worldly concerns, that it used to be one of the chief cares of Satish to look after him and keep him safe from disaster. Thus had Satish received from and given to his uncle his all.

What the bleakness of his bereavement meant for Satish, it was impossible for us to conceive. He struggled against the agony of negation, refusing to believe that such absolute blankness could be true: that there could be emptiness so desolate as to be void even of Truth. If that which seemed one vast 'No' had not also its aspect of 'Yes,' would not the whole universe leak away through its yawning gap into nothingness?

For two years Satish wandered from place to place, we had no touch with him. We threw ourselves with all the greater zeal into our self appointed tasks. We made it a special point to shock those who professed belief in any kind of religion, and the fields of good work we selected were such that not a good soul had a good word left for us. Satish had been our flower; when he dropped off, we, the thorns, cast off our sheaths and gloried in our sharpness.

Two years had passed since we lost sight of Satish. My mind revolted against harbouring the least thing evil against him, nevertheless I could not help suspecting that the high pitch at which he used to be kept strung must have been flattened down by this shock.

Uncle Jagamohan had once said of a Sannyasin: 'As the money-changer tests the ring of each coin, so does the world test each man by the response he gives to shocks of loss and pain, and the resistance he offers to the craze for cheap salvation. Those who fail to ring true are cast aside as worthless. These wandering ascetics have been so rejected, as being unfit to take part in the world's commerce, yet the vagabonds swagger about, boasting that it is they who have renounced the world! The worthy are permitted no loophole of escape from duty, only withered leaves are allowed to fall off the tree.'

Had it come to this, that Satish, of all people, had joined the ranks of the withered and the worthless? Was he, then, fated to leave on the black touchstone of bereavement his mark of spuriousness?

While assailed with these misgivings, news suddenly reached us that Satish (our Satish, if you please!) was making the heavens resound with his cymbals in some out-of-the-way village, singing frenzied kirtans [Footnote: The kirtan is a kind of devotional oratorio sung to the accompaniment of drums and cymbals, the libretto ranging over the whole gamut of human emotions, which are made the vehicle for communion with the Divine Lover. As their feelings get worked up, the singers begin to sway their bodies with, and finally dance to, the rhythm.] as a follower of Lilananda Swami, the Vaishnava revivalist!

It had passed my comprehension, when I first began to know Satish, how he could ever have come to be an atheist. I was now equally at a loss to understand how Lilananda Swami could have managed to lead him such a dance with his kirtans.

And how on earth were we to show our faces? What laughter there would be in the camp of the enemy, whose number, thanks to our folly, was legion! Our band waxed mightily wroth with Satish. Many of them said they had known from the very first that there was no rational substance in him, he was all frothy idealism. And I now discovered how much I really loved Satish. He had dealt his ardent sect of atheists their deathblow, yet I could not be angry with him.

Off I started to hunt up Lilananda Swami. River after river I crossed, and trudged over endless fields. The nights I spent in grocers' shops. At last in one of the villages I came up against Satish's party.

It was then two o'clock in the afternoon. I had been hoping to catch Satish alone. Impossible! The cottage which was honoured with the Swami's presence was packed all round with crowds of his disciples. There had been kirtans all the morning; those who had come from a distance were now waiting to have their meal served.

As soon as Satish caught sight of me, he dashed up and embraced me fervidly. I was staggered. Satish had always been extremely reserved. His outward calm had been the only measure of his depth of feeling. He now appeared as though intoxicated.

The Swami was resting in the front room, with the door ajar. He could see us. At once came the call, in a deep voice: 'Satish!'

Satish was back inside, all in a flurry.

'Who is that?' inquired the Swami.

'Srivilas, a great friend of mine,' Satish reported.

During these years I had managed to make a name for myself in our little world. A learned Englishman had remarked, on hearing one of my English speeches: 'The man has a wonderful -.' But let that be. Why add to the number of my enemies? Suffice it to say that, from the students up to the students' grandparents, the reputation had travelled round that I was a rampaging atheist who could bestride the English language and race her over the hurdles at breakneck speed in the most marvellous manner.

I somehow felt that the Swami was pleased to have me here. He sent for me. I merely hinted at the usual salutation as I entered his room, that is to say, my joined hands were uplifted, but my head was not lowered.

This did not escape the Swami. 'Here, Satish!' he ordered. 'Fill me that pipe of mine.'

Satish set to work. But as he lit the tinder, it was I who was set ablaze within. Moreover, I was getting fidgety, not knowing where to sit. The only seat in the room was a wooden bedstead on which was spread the Swami's carpet. Not that I confessed to any qualms about occupying a corner of the same carpet on which the great man was installed, but somehow my sitting down did not come off. I remained standing near the door.

It appeared that the Swami was aware of my having won the Premchand-Roychand [Footnote: The highest prize at the Calcutta University. scholarship.] 'My son,' he said to me, 'it is good for the pearl diver if he succeeds in reaching the bottom, but he would die if he had to stay there. He must come up for the free breath of life. If you would live, you must now come up to the light, out of the depths of your learning. You have enjoyed the fruits of your scholarship, now try a taste of the joys of its renunciation.'

Satish handed his Master the lighted pipe and sat down on the bare floor near his feet. The Swami leant back and stretched his legs out towards Satish, who began gently to massage them. This was more than I could stand. I left the room. I could, of course, see that this ordering about of Satish and making him fetch and carry was deliberately directed at me.

The Swami went on resting. All the guests were duly served by the householder with a meal of kedgeree. From five o'clock the kirtans started again and went on till ten in the night.

When I got Satish alone at last, I said to him: 'Look here, Satish! You have been brought up in the atmosphere of freedom from infancy. How have you managed to get yourself entangled in this kind of bondage to-day? Is Uncle Jagamohan, then, so utterly dead?'

Partly because the playfulness of affection prompted it, partly, perhaps, because precision of description required it, Satish used to reverse the first two syllables of my name and call me Visri. [Footnote: Ungainly, ugly.]

'Visri,' he replied, 'while Uncle was alive he gave me freedom in life's field of work, the freedom which the child gets in the playground. After his death it is he, again, who has given me freedom on the high seas of emotion, the freedom which the child gains when it comes back to its mother's arms. I have enjoyed to the full the freedom of life's day-time; why should I now deprive myself of the freedom of its evening?

Be sure that both these are the gift of that same uncle of ours.'

'Whatever you may say,' I persisted, 'Uncle could have nothing to do with this kind of pipe-filling, leg-massaging business. Surely this is no picture of freedom.'

'That,' argued Satish, 'was the freedom on shore. There Uncle gave full liberty of action to our limbs. This is freedom on the ocean. Here the confinement of the ship is necessary for our progress. That is why my Master keeps me bound to his service. This massaging is helping me to cross over.'

'It does not sound so bad,' I admitted,'the way you put it. But, all the same, I have no patience with a man who can thrust out his legs at you like that.'

'He can do it,' explained Satish, 'because he has no need of such service. Had it been for himself, he might have felt ashamed to ask it. The need is mine.'

I realised that the world into which Satish had been transported had no place for me, his particular friend. The person, whom Satish has so effusively embraced, was not Srivilas, but a representative of all humanity, just an idea. Such ideas are like wine. When they get into the head any one can be embraced and wept over I, only as much as anybody else. But whatever joys may be the portion of the ecstatic one, what can such embrace signify to me, the other party? What satisfaction am I to get, merely to be accounted one of the ripples on a grand, difference-obliterating flood, I, the individual I?

However, further argument was clearly useless. Nor could I make up my mind to desert Satish. So, as his satellite, I also danced from village to village, carried along the current of kirtan singing.

The intoxication of it gradually took hold of me. I also embraced all and sundry, wept without provocation, and tended the feet of the Master. And one day, in a moment of curious exaltation, Satish was revealed to me in a light for which there can be no other name than divine.

IV

With the capture of two such egregious, college-educated atheists as we were, the fame of Lilananda Swami spread far and wide. His Calcutta disciples now pressed him to take up his headquarters at the metropolis.

So Swami Lilananda came on to Calcutta. Shivatosh had been a devoted follower of Lilananda. Whenever the Swami visited Calcutta he had stayed with Shivatosh. And it was the one delight of Shivatosh's life to serve the Master, together with all his disciples, when they thus honoured his house. When he died he bequeathed all his property to the Swami, leaving only a life-interest in the income to his young childless widow. It was his hope that this house of his would become a pilgrim-centre for the sect.

This was the house where we now went into residence.

During our ecstatic progress through the villages I had been in an elated mood, which I now found it difficult to keep up in Calcutta. In the wonderland of emotion, where we had been revelling, the mystic drama of the courting of the Bride within us and the Bridegroom who is everywhere was being played. And a fitting accompaniment to it had been the symphony of the broad grazing greens, the shaded ferry landing-places, the enraptured expanse of the noonday leisure, the deep evening silences vibrant with the tremolo of cicadas. Ours had been a dream progress to which the open skies of the countryside offered no obstacle. But with our arrival at Calcutta we knocked our heads against its hardness, we got jostled by its crowds, and our dream was at an end.

Yet, was not this the same Calcutta where, within the confines of our students' lodgings, we had once put our whole soul into our studies, by day and by night; where we had pondered over and discussed the problems of our country with our fellow-students in the College Square; where we had served as volunteers at the holding of our National Assemblies; where we had responded to the call of Uncle Jagamohan, and taken the vow to free our minds from all slavery imposed by Society or State? Yes, it was in this self-same Calcutta that, in the flood-tide of our youth, we had pursued our course, regardless of the revilement of stranger and kindred alike, proudly breasting all contrary currents like a boat in full sail. Why, then, should we now fail, in this whirlpool of suffering humanity, ridden with pleasure and pain, driven by hunger and thirst, to keep up the exaltation proper to our tear-drenched cult of emotional Communion?

As I manfully made the attempt, I was beset with doubts at every step. Was I then a mere weakling: unfaithful to my ideal: unworthy of strenuous endeavour? When I turned to Satish, to see how he fared, I found on his countenance no sign to show that Calcutta, for him, represented any geographical reality whatsoever. In the mystic world where he dwelt, all this city life meant no more than a mirage.

V

We two friends took up our quarters, with the Master, in Shivatosh's house. We had come to be his chief disciples, and he would have us constantly near his person.

With our Master and our fellow-disciples we were absorbed day and night in discussing emotions in general and the philosophy of spiritual emotion in particular. Into the very thick of the abstruse complexities which thus engaged our attention, the ripple of a woman's laughter would now and again find its way from the inner apartments. [Footnote: The women's part of the house.] Sometimes there would be heard, in a clear, high-toned voice, the call 'Bami!' evidently a maid-servant of that name.

These were doubtless but trivial interruptions for minds soaring, almost to vanishing point, into the empyrean of idea. But to me they came as a grateful shower of rain upon a parched and thirsty soil. When little touches of life, like shed flower petals, were blown across from the unknown world behind the wall, then all in a moment I could understand that the wonderland of our quest was just there, where the keys jingled, tied to the corner of Bami's sari; where the sound of the broom rose from the swept floor, and the smell of the cooking from the kitchen, all trifles, but all true. That world, with its mingling of fine and coarse, bitter and sweet, that itself was the heaven where Emotion truly held sway.

The name of the widow was Damini. We could catch momentary glimpses of her through opening doors and flapping curtains. But the two of us grew to be so much part and parcel of the Master as to share his privilege, [Footnote: Women do not observe purdah with religious ascetics.] and very soon these doors and curtains were no longer barriers in our case.

Damini [Footnote: Damini means Lightning.] was the lightning which gleams within the massed clouds of July. Without, the curves of youth enveloped her in their fulness, within flashed fitful fires. Thus runs an entry in Satish's diary:

In Nonibala I have seen the Universal Woman in one of her aspects, the woman who takes on herself the whole burden of sin, who gives up life itself for the sinner's sake, and in dying leaves for the world the balm of immortality. In Damini I see another aspect of Universal Woman. This one has nothing to do with death, she is the Artist of the Art of Life. She blossoms out, in limitless profusion, in form and scent and movement. She is not for rejection; refuses to entertain the ascetic; and is vowed to resist the least farthing of payment to the tax-gathering Winter Wind.

It is necessary to relate Damini's previous history.

At the time when the coffers of her father, Annada, were overflowing with proceeds of his jute business, Damini was married to Shivatosh. So long, Shivatosh's fortune had consisted only in his pedigree: it could now count a more substantial addition. Annada bestowed on his son-in-law a house in Calcutta and sufficient money to keep him for life. There were also lavish gifts of furniture and ornaments made to his daughter.

Annada, further, made a futile attempt to take Shivatosh into his own business. But the latter had no interest in worldly concerns. An astrologer had once predicted to Shivatosh that, on the happening of a special conjunction of the stars, his soul would gain its emancipation whilst still in the flesh. From that day he lived in this hope alone, and ceased to find charm in riches, or even in objects still more charming. It was while in this frame of mind that he had become a disciple of Lilananda Swami.

In the meantime, with the subsidence of the jute boom, the full force of the adverse wind caught the heavy-laden bark of Annada's fortune and toppled it over. All his property was sold up and he had hardly enough left to make a bare living.

One evening Shivatosh came into the inner apartments and said to his wife: 'The Master is here. He has some words of advice for you and bids you attend.'

'I cannot go to him now,' answered Damini. 'I haven't the time.'

What? No time! Shivatosh went up nearer and found his wife seated in the gathering dusk, in front of the open safe, with her ornaments spread out before her. 'What in the world is keeping you?' inquired he.

'I am arranging my jewels,' was the reply.

So that was the reason for her lack of time. Indeed!

The next day, when Damini opened the safe, she found her jewel-box missing. 'My jewels?' she exclaimed, turning inquiringly to her husband.

'But you offered them to the Master. Did not his call reach you at the very moment? for he sees into the minds of men. He has deigned, in his mercy, to save you from the lure of pelf.'

Damini's indignation rose to white heat.

'Give me back my ornaments!' she commanded.

'Why, what will you do with them?'

'They were my father's gift to me. I would return them to him.'

'They have gone to a better place,' said Shivatosh. 'Instead of pandering to worldly needs they are dedicated to the service of devotees.'

That is how the tyrannical imposition of faith began. And the pious ritual of exorcism, in all its cruelty, continued to be practised in order to rid Damini's mind of its mundane affections and desires.

So, while her father and her little brother were starving by inches, Damini had to prepare daily, with her own hands, meals for the sixty or seventy disciples who thronged the house with the Master. She would sometimes rebelliously leave out the salt, or contrive to get the viands scorched, but that did not avail to gain her any respite from her penance.

At this juncture Shivatosh died: and in departing he awarded his wife the supreme penalty for her want of faith, he committed his widow, with all her belongings, to the guardianship of the Master.

VI

The house was in a constant tumult with rising waves of fervour. Devotees kept streaming in from all quarters to sit at the feet of the Master. And yet Damini, who had gained the Presence without effort of her own, thrust aside her good fortune with contumely.

Did the Master call her for some special mark of his favour she would keep aloof, pleading a headache. If he had occasion to complain of some special omission of personal attention on her part, she would confess to have been away at the theatre. The excuse was lacking in truth, but not in rudeness.

The other women disciples were aghast at Damini's ways. First, her attire was not such as widows [Footnote: Hindu widows in Bengal are supposed to dress in simple white (sometimes plain brown silk), without border, or ornamentation.] should affect. Secondly, she showed no eagerness to drink in the Master's words of wisdom. Lastly, her demeanour had none of the reverential restraint which the Master's presence demanded. 'What a shame,' exclaimed they. 'We have seen many awful women, but not one so outrageous.'

The Swami used to smile. 'The Lord,' said he,'takes a special delight in wrestling with a valiant opponent. When Damini has to own defeat, her surrender will be absolute.'

He began to display an exaggerated tolerance for her contumacy. That vexed Damini still more, for she looked on it as a more cunning form of punishment. And one day the Master caught her in a fit of laughter, mimicking to one of her companions the excessive suavity of his manner towards herself. Still he had not a word of rebuke, and repeated simply that the final denouement would be all the more extraordinary, to which end the poor thing was but the instrument of Providence, and so herself not to blame.

This was how we found her when we first came. The denouement was indeed extraordinary. I can hardly bring myself to write on further. Moreover, what happened is so difficult to tell. The network of suffering, which is woven behind the scenes, is not of any pattern set by the Scriptures, nor of our own devising. Hence the frequent discords between the inner and the outer life, discords that hurt, and wail forth in tears.

There came, at length, the dawn when the harsh crust of rebelliousness cracked and fell to pieces, and the flower of self-surrender came through and held up its dew-washed face. Damini's service became so beautiful in its truth that it descended on the devotees like the blessing of the very Divinity of their devotions.

And when Damini's lightning flashes had matured into a steady radiance, Satish looked on her and saw that she was beautiful; but I say this, that Satish gazed only on her beauty, failing to see Damini herself.

In Satish's room there hung a portrait of the Swami sitting in meditation, done on a porcelain medallion. One day he found it on the floor, in fragments. He put it down to his pet cat.

But other little mischiefs began to follow, which were clearly beyond the powers of the cat. There was some kind of disturbance in the air, which now and again broke out in unseen electric shocks.

How others felt, I know not, but a growing pain gnawed at my heart. Sometimes I thought that this constant ecstasy of emotion was proving too much for me. I wanted to give it all up and run away. The old work of teaching the leather-dealers' children seemed, in its unalloyed prose, to be now calling me back.

One afternoon when the Master was taking his siesta, and the weary disciples were at rest, Satish for some reason went off into his own room at this unusual hour. His progress was suddenly arrested at the threshold. There was Damini, her thick tresses dishevelled, lying prone on the floor, beating her head on it as she moaned: 'Oh, you stone, you stone, have mercy on me, have mercy and kill me outright!'

Satish, trembling from head to foot with a nameless fear, fled from the room.

VII

It was a rule with Swami Lilananda to go off once a year to some remote, out-of-the-way place, away from the crowd. With the month of Magh [Footnote: January-February.] came round the time for his journey. Satish was to attend on him.

I asked to go too. I was worn to the very bone with the incessant emotional excitement of our cult, and felt greatly in need of physical movement as well as of mental quiet.

The Master sent for Damini. 'My little mother,' he told her, 'I am about to leave you for the duration of my travels. Let me arrange for your stay meanwhile with your aunt, as usual.'

'I would accompany you,' said Damini.

'You could hardly bear it, I am afraid. Our journeying will be troublesome.'

'Of course I can bear it,' she answered. 'Pray have no concern about any trouble of mine.'

Lilananda was pleased at this proof of Damini's devotion. In former years, this opportunity had been Damini's holiday time, the one thing to which she had looked forward through the preceding months. 'Miraculous!' thought the Swami. 'How wondrously does even stone become as wax in the Lord's melting-pot of emotion.'

So Damini had her way, and came along with us.

VIII

The spot we reached, after hours of tramping in the sun, was a little promontory on the sea-coast, shaded by cocoa-nut palms. Profound was the solitude and the tranquillity which reigned there, as the gentle rustle of the palm tassels merged into the idle plash of the girdling sea. The place looked like a tired hand of the sleepy shore, limply fallen upon the surface of the waters. On this open hand stood a bluish-green hill, and inside the hill was a sculptured cave-temple of bygone days, which, for all its serene beauty, was the cause of much disquiet amongst antiquarians as to the origin, style, and subject-matter of its sculptures.

Our intention had been to return to the village where we had made our halt, after paying a visit to this temple. That was now seen to be impossible. The day was fast declining, and the moon was long past its full. Lilananda Swami at length decided that we should pass the night in the cave.

All four of us sat down to rest on the sandy soil beneath the cocoa-nut groves fringing the sea. The sunset glow bent lower and lower over the western horizon, as though Day was making its parting obeisance to approaching Night.

The Master's voice broke forth in song, one of his own composition:

  The day has waned, when at last we meet at the turning;

  And as I try to see thy face, the last ray of evening fades into the night.

We had heard the song before, but never with such complete rapport between singer, audience, and surroundings. Damini was affected to tears. The Swami went on to the second verse:

  I shall not grieve that the darkness comes between thee and my sight,

  Only, for a moment, stand before me, that I may kiss thy feet and wipe them with my hair.

When he had come to the end, the placid eventide, enveloping sky and waters, was filled, like some ripe, golden fruit, with the bursting sweetness of melody.

Damini rose and went up to the Master. As she prostrated herself at his feet, her loose hair slipped off her shoulders and was scattered over the ground on either side. She remained long thus before she raised her head.

IX

(FROM SATISH'S DIARY)

There were several chambers within the temple. In one of these I spread my blanket and laid myself down. The darkness pent up inside the cave seemed alive, like some great black monster, its damp breath bedewing my body. I began to be haunted by the idea that this was the first of all created animals, born in the beginning of time, with no eyes or ears, but just one enormous appetite. Confined within this cavern for endless ages it knew nothing, having no mind; but having sensibility it felt; and wept and wept in silence.

Fatigue overpowered my limbs like a dead weight, but sleep came not. Some bird, or perhaps bat, flitted in from the outside, or out from the inside, its wings beating the air as it flew from darkness to darkness; when the draught reached my body it sent a shiver through me, making my flesh creep.

I thought I would go and get some sleep outside. But I could not recollect the direction in which the entrance was. As I crawled on my hands and knees along the way which appeared the right one, I knocked against the cave wall. When I tried a different side, I nearly tumbled into a hollow in which the water dripping through the cracks had collected.

I crawled back to my blanket and stretched myself on it again. Again was I possessed with the fancy that I had been taken right into the creature's maw and could not extricate myself; that I was the victim of a blind hunger which was licking me with its slimy saliva, through which I would be sucked and digested noiselessly, little by little.

I felt that only sleep could save me. My living, waking consciousness was evidently unable to bear such close embrace of this horrible, suffocating obscurity, fit only for the dead to suffer. I cannot say how long after it came upon me, or whether it was really sleep at all, but a thin veil of oblivion fell at last over my senses. And while in such half-conscious state I actually felt a deep breathing somewhere near my bare feet. Surely it was not that primeval creature of my imagining!

Then something seemed to cling about my feet. Some real wild animal this time, was my first thought. But there was nothing furry in its touch. What if it was some species of serpent or reptile, of features and body unknown to me, of whose method of absorbing its prey I could form no idea? All the more loathsome seemed the softness of it, of this terrible, unknown mass of hunger.

What between dread and disgust, I could not even utter a cry. I tried to push it away with ineffectual thrusts with my legs. Its face seemed to be touching my feet, on which its panting breath fell thickly. What kind of a face had it, I wondered. I launched a more vigorous kick as the stupor left me. I had at first supposed there was no fur, but what felt like a mane now brushed across my legs. I struggled up into a sitting posture.

Something stole away in the darkness. There was also a curious kind of sound. Could it have been sobbing?

CHAPTER III

DAMINI

I

We are back in our quarters in the village, near a temple, in a two-storeyed house belonging to one of the Swami's disciples, which had been placed at our disposal. Since our return we see but little of Damini, though she is still in charge of our household affairs. She has made friends with the neighbouring women, and spends most of her spare time in going about with them from one house to another.

The Swami is not particularly pleased. Damini's heart, thinks he, does not yet respond to the call of the ethereal heights. All its fondness is still for earthen walls. In her daily work of looking after the devotees, formerly like an act of worship with her, a trace of weariness has become noticeable. She makes mistakes. Her service has lost its radiance.

The Master, at heart, begins to be afraid of her again. Between her brows there darkens a gathering frown; her temple is ruffled with fitful breezes; the loosening knot of her hair lowers over her neck; the pressure of her lips, the gleams from the corner of her eye, her sudden wayward gestures presage a rebellious storm.

The Swami turned to his kirtans with renewed attention. The wandering bee, he hoped, would be brought to drink deep of the honey, once enticed in by its fragrance. And so the short cool days were filled to the brim with the foaming wine of ecstatic song.

But no, Damini refused to be caught. The exasperated Swami laughed out one day: 'The Lord is out hunting: the resolute flight of the deer adds zest to the chase: but succumb she must, in the end.'

When we had first come to know Damini, she was not to be found among the band of devotees clustering round the Master. That, however, did not attract our notice then. But now, her empty place had become conspicuous. Her frequent absences smote us tempestuously.

The Swami put this down to her pride, and that hurt his own pride. As for me, but what does it matter what I thought?

One day the Master mustered up courage to say in his most dulcet tones: 'Damini, my little mother, do you think you will have a little time to spare this afternoon? If so -'

'No,' said Damini.

'Would you mind telling me why?',

'I have to assist in making sweetmeats at the Nandi's.'

'Sweetmeats? What for?'

'They have a wedding on.'

'Is your assistance so indispensably -?'

'I promised to be there.'

Damini whisked out of the room without waiting for further questioning.

Satish, who was there with us, was dumbfounded. So many men of learning, wealth, and fame had surrendered at the feet of the Master, and this slip of a girl, what gave her such hardihood of assurance?

Another evening Damini happened to be at home. The Master had addressed himself to some specially important topic. After his discourse had progressed awhile, something in our faces gave him pause. He found our attention wandering. On looking round he discovered that Damini, who had been seated in the room, sewing in hand, was not to be seen. He understood the reason of our distraction. She was not there, not there, not there, the refrain now kept worrying him too. He began to lose the thread of his discourse, and at last gave it up altogether.

The Swami left the room and went off to Damini's door. 'Damini,' he called. 'Why are you all alone here? Will you not come and join us?'

'I am engaged,' said Damini.

The baffled Swami could see, as he passed by the half-open door, a captive kite in a cage. It had somehow struck against the telegraph wires, and had been lying wounded when Damini rescued it from the pestering crows, and she had been tending it since.

The kite was not the only object which engaged Damini's solicitude. There was a mongrel pup, whose looks were on a par with its breeding. It was discord personified. Whenever it heard our cymbals, it would look up to heaven and voice forth a prolonged complaint. The gods, being fortunate, did not feel bound to give it a hearing. The poor mortals whose ears happened to be within reach were woefully agonised.

One afternoon, when Damini was engaged in practising horticulture in sundry cracked pots on the roof-terrace, Satish came up and asked her point-blank: 'Why is it you have given up coming over there altogether?'

'Over where?'

'To the Master.'

'Why, what need have you people of me?'

'We have no need, but surely the need is yours.'

'No, no!' flung out Damini. 'Not at all, not at all!'

Taken aback by her heat, Satish gazed at her in silence. Then he mused aloud: 'Your mind lacks peace. If you would gain peace -'

'Peace from you, you who are consumed day and night with your excitement, where have you the peace to give? Leave me alone, I beg and pray you. I was at peace. I would be at peace.'

'You see but the waves on the surface. If you have the patience to dive deep, you will find all calm there.'

Damini wrung her hands as she cried: 'I beseech you, for the Lord's sake, don't insist on my diving downwards. If only you will give up all hope of my conversion, I may yet live.'

II

My experience has never been large enough to enable me to penetrate the mysteries of woman's mind. Judging from what little I have seen of the surface from the outside, I have come to the belief that women are ever ready to bestow their heart where sorrow cannot but be their lot. They will either string their garland of acceptance [Footnote: In the old days, when a girl had to choose between several suitors, she signified her choice by putting a garland round the neck of the accepted one.] for some brute of a man who will trample it under foot and defile it in the mire of his passions, or dedicate it to some idealist, on whose neck it will get no hold, attenuated as he is, like the dream-stuff of his imaginings.

When left to do their own choosing, women invariably reject ordinary men like me, made up of gross and fine, who know woman to be just woman, that is to say, neither a doll of clay made to serve for our pastime, nor a transcendental melody to be evoked at our master touch. They reject us, because we have neither the forceful delusions of the flesh, nor the roseate illusions of fancy: we can neither break them on the wheel of our desire, nor melt them in the glow of our fervour to be cast in the mould of our ideal.

Because we know them only for what they are, they may be friendly, but cannot love us. We are their true refuge, for they can rely on our devotion; but our self-dedication comes so easy that they forget it has a price. So the only reward we get is to be used for their purposes; perchance to win their respect. But I am afraid my excursions into the region of psychology are merely due to personal grievances, which have my own experience behind them. The fact probably is, what we thus lose is really our gain, anyway, that is how we may console ourselves.

Damini avoids the Master because she cannot bear him. She fights shy of Satish because for him her feelings are of the opposite description. I am the only person, near at hand, with whom there is no question either of love or hate. So whenever I am with her, Damini talks away to me of unimportant matters concerning the old days, the present times, or the daily happenings at the neighbours' houses. These talks usually take place on the shaded part of the roof-terrace, which serves as a passage between our several rooms on the second storey, where Damini sits slicing betel-nuts.

What I could not understand was, how these trifling talks should have attracted the notice of Satish's emotion-clouded vision. Even suppose the circumstance was not so trifling, had I not often been told that, in the world where Satish dwelt, there were no such disturbing things as circumstances at all? The Mystic Union, in which personified cosmic forces were assisting, was an eternal drama, not an historical episode. Those who are rapt with the undying flute strains, borne along by the ceaseless zephyrs which play on the banks of the ever-flowing Jamuna of that mystic paradise, have no eyes or ears left for the ephemeral doings immediately around them. This much at least is certain, that before our return from the cave, Satish used to be much denser in his perception of worldly events.

For this difference I may have been partly responsible. I also had begun to absent myself from our kirtans and discourses, perhaps with a frequency which could not elude even Satish. One day he came round on inquiry, and found me running after Damini's mongoose, a recent acquisition, trying to lure it into bondage with a pot of milk, which I had procured from the local milkman. This occupation, viewed as an excuse, was simply hopeless. It could easily have waited till the end of our sitting. For the matter of that, the best thing clearly would have been to leave the mongoose to its own devices, thus at one stroke demonstrating my adherence to the two principal tenets of our cult, Compassion for all creatures, and Passion for the Lord.

That is why, when Satish came up, I had to feel ashamed. I put down the pot, then and there, and tried to edge away along the path which led back to self-respect.

But Damini's behaviour took me by surprise. She was not in the least abashed as she asked: 'Where are you off to, Srivilas Babu?'

I scratched my head, as I mumbled: 'I was thinking of joining the -'

'They must have finished by this time. Do sit down.'

This coming from Damini, in the presence of Satish, made my ears burn.

Damini turned to Satish. 'I am in awful trouble with the mongoose,' she said. 'Last night it stole a chicken from the Mussulman quarters over there. I dare not leave it loose any longer. Srivilas Babu has promised to look out for a nice big hamper to keep it in.'

It seemed to me that it was my devotion to her which Damini was using the mongoose to show off. I was reminded how the Swami had given orders to Satish so as to impress me. The two were the same thing.

Satish made no reply, and his departure was somewhat abrupt. I gazed on Damini and could see her eyes flash out as they followed his disappearing figure; while on her lips there set a hard, enigmatic smile.

What conclusion Damini had come to she herself knew best; the only result apparent to me was that she began to send for me on all kinds of flimsy pretexts. Sometimes she would make sweetmeats, which she pressed on me. One day I could not help suggesting: 'Let's offer some to Satish as well.'

'That would only annoy him,' said Damini.

And it happened that Satish, passing that way, caught me in the act of being thus regaled.

In the drama which was being played, the hero and the heroine spoke their parts 'aside.' I was the one character who, being of no consequence, had to speak out. This sometimes made me curse my lot; none the less, I could not withstand the temptation of the petty cash with which I was paid off, from day to day, for taking up the role of middleman.

III

For some days Satish clanged his cymbals and danced his kirtans with added vigour. Then one day he came to me and said: 'We cannot keep Damini with us any longer.'

'Why?' I asked.

'We must free ourselves altogether from the influence of women.'

'If that be a necessity,' said I,'there must be something radically wrong with our system.'

Satish stared at me in amazement.

'Woman is a natural phenomenon,' I continued, undaunted, 'who will have her place in the world, however much we may try to get rid of her. If your spiritual welfare depends on ignoring her existence, then its pursuit will be like the chasing of a phantom, and will so put you to shame, when the illusion is gone, that you will not know where to hide yourself.'

'Oh, stop your philosophising!' exclaimed Satish. 'I was talking practical politics. It is only too evident that women are emissaries of Maya, and at Maya's behest ply on us their blandishments, for they cannot fulfil the design of their Mistress unless they overpower our reason. So we must steer clear of them if we would keep our intellect free.'

I was about to make my reply, when Satish stopped me with a gesture, and went on: 'Visri, old fellow! let me tell you plainly: if the hand of Maya is not visible to you, that is because you have allowed yourself to be caught in her net. The vision of beauty with which she has ensnared you to-day will vanish, and with the beauty will disappear the spectacles of desire, through which you now see it as greater than all the world. Where the noose of Maya is so glaringly obvious, why be foolhardy enough to take risks?'

'I admit all that,' I rejoined. 'But, my dear fellow, the all-pervading net of Maya was not cast by my hands, nor do I know the way to escape through it. Since we have not the power to evade Maya, our spiritual striving should help us, while acknowledging her, to rise above her. Because it does not take such a course, we have to flounder about in vain attempts to cut away the half of Truth.'

'Well, well, let's have your idea a little more clearly,' said Satish.

'We must sail the boat of our life,' I proceeded, 'along the current of nature, in order to reach beyond it. Our problem is, not how to get rid of this current, but how to keep the boat afloat in its channel until it is through. For that, a rudder is necessary.'

'You people who have ceased to be loyal to the Master, how can I make you understand that in him we have just this rudder? You would regulate your spiritual life according to your own whims. That way death lies!' Satish went to the Master's chamber, and fell to tending his feet with fervour.

The same evening, when Satish lit the Master's pipe, he also put forward his plaint against Maya and her emissaries. The smoking of one pipe, however, did not suffice for its adjudication. Evening after evening, pipe after pipe was exhausted, yet the Master was unable to make up his mind.

>From the very beginning Damini had given the Swami no end of trouble. Now the girl had managed to set up this eddy in the midst of the smooth course of the devotees' progress. But Shivatosh had thrown her and her belongings so absolutely on the Master's hands that he knew not how or where to cast her off. What made it more difficult still was that he harboured a secret fear of his ward.

And Satish, in spite of all the doubled and quadrupled enthusiasm which he put into his kirtans, in spite of all the pipe-filling and massaging in which he tried to rest his heart, was not allowed to forget for a moment that Maya had taken up her position right across the line of his spiritual advance.

One day some kirtan singers of repute had arrived, and were to sing in the evening at the temple next door. The kirtan would last far into the night. I managed to slip away after the preliminary overture, having no doubt that, in so thick a crowd, no one would notice my absence.

Damini that evening had completely thrown off her reserve. Things which are difficult to speak of, which refuse to leave one's choking throat, flowed from her lips so simply, so sweetly. It was as if she had suddenly come upon some secret recess in her heart, so long hidden away in darkness, as if, by some strange chance, she had gained the opportunity to stand before her own self, face to face.

Just at this time Satish came up from behind and stood there hesitating, without our being aware of it at the moment. Not that Damini was saying anything very particular, but there were tears in her eyes, all her words, in fact, were then welling up from some tear-flooded depth. When Satish arrived, the kirtan could not have been anywhere near its end. I divined that he must have been goaded with repeated inward urgings to have left the temple then.

As Satish came round into our view, Damini rose with a start, wiped her eyes, and made off towards her room. Satish, with a tremor in his voice, said: 'Damini, will you listen to me? I would have a word with you.'

Damini slowly retraced her steps, and came and sat down again. I made as though to take myself off, but an imploring glance from her restrained me from stirring. Satish, who seemed to have made some kind of effort meanwhile, came straight to the point.

'The need,' said he to Damini, 'which brought the rest of us to the Master, was not yours when you came to him.'

'No,' avowed Damini expectantly.

'Why, then, do you stay amongst his devotees?'

Damini's eyes flamed up as she cried: 'Why do I stay? Because I did not come of my own accord! I was a helpless creature, and everyone knew my lack of faith. Yet I was bound hand and foot by your devotees in this dungeon of devotion. What avenue of escape have you left me?'

'We have now decided,' stated Satish,'that if you would go to stay with some relative all your expenses will be found.'

'You have decided, have you?'

'Yes.'

'Well, then, I have not!'

'Why, how will that inconvenience you?'

'Am I a pawn in your game, that you devotees should play me, now this way, now the other?'

Satish was struck dumb.

'I did not come,' continued Damini, 'wanting to please your devotees. And I am not going away at the bidding of the lot of you, merely because I don't happen to please you!'

Damini covered her face with her hands and burst out sobbing as she ran into her room and slammed the door.

Satish did not return to the kirtan singing. He sank down in a corner of the adjoining roof-terrace and brooded there in silence.

The sound of the breakers on the distant seashore came, wafted along the south breeze, like despairing sighs, rising up to the watching star clusters, from the very heart of the Earth. I spent the night wandering round and round along the dark, deserted village lanes.

IV

The World of Reality has made a determined onslaught on the Mystic Paradise, within the confines of which the Master sought to keep Satish and myself content by repeatedly filling for us the cup of symbolism with the nectar of idea. Now the clash of the actual with the symbolic bids fair to overturn the latter and spill its emotional contents in the dust. The Master is not blind to this danger.

Satish is no longer himself. Like a paper kite, with its regulating knot gone, he is still high in the skies, but may at any moment begin to gyrate groundwards. There is no falling off as yet in the outward rigour of his devotional and disciplinary exercises, but a closer scrutiny reveals the totter of weakening.

As for my condition, Damini has left nothing so vague in it as to require any guess-work. The more she notices the fear in the Master's face, and the pain in Satish's, the oftener she makes me dance attendance on her.

At last it came to this, that when we were engaged in talk with the Master, Damini would sometimes appear in the doorway and interrupt us with: 'Srivilas Babu, would you mind coming over this way?' without even condescending to add what I was wanted for.

The Swami would glance up at me; Satish would glance up at me; I would hesitate for a moment between them and her; then I would glance up at the door, and in a trice I was off the fence and out of the room. An effort would be made, after my exit, to go on with the talk, but the effort would soon get the better of the talk, whereupon the latter would stop.

Everything seemed to be falling to pieces around us. The old compactness was gone.

We two had come to be the pillars of the sect. The Master could not give up either of us without a struggle. So he ventured once more to make an overture to Damini. 'My little mother,' said he,'the time is coming for us to proceed to the more arduous part of our journey. You had better return from here.'

'Return where?'

'Home, to your aunt.'

'That cannot be.'

'Why?' asked the Swami. 'First of all,' said Damini,'she is not my own aunt at all. Why should she bear my burden?'

'All your expenses shall be borne by us.'

'Expenses are not the only burden. It is no part of her duty to be saddled with looking after me.'

'But, Damini,' urged the Swami in his desperation, 'can I keep you with me for ever?'

'Is that a question for me to answer?'

'But where will you go when I am dead?'

'I was never allowed,' returned Damini icily, 'to have the responsibility of thinking that out. I have been made to realise too well that in this world I have neither home nor property; nothing at all to call my own. That is what makes my burden so heavy to bear. It pleased you to take it up. You shall not now cast it on another!'

Damini went off.

'Lord, have mercy!' sighed the Swami.

Damini had laid on me the command to procure for her some good Bengali books. I need hardly say that by 'good' Damini did not mean spiritual, of the quality affected by our sect. Nor need I pause to make it clear that Damini had no compunction in asking anything from me. It had not taken her long to find out that making demands on me was the easiest way of making me amends. Some kinds of trees are all the better for being pruned: that was the kind of person I seemed to be where Damini was concerned.

Well, the books I ordered were unmitigatedly modern. The author was distinctly less influenced by Manu [Footnote: The Hindu law-giver.] than by Man himself. The packet was delivered by the postman to the Swami. He raised his eyebrows, as he opened it, and asked: 'Hullo, Srivilas, what are these for?'

I remained silent.

The Master gingerly turned over some of the pages, as he remarked for my benefit that he had never thought much of the author, having failed to find in his writings the correct spiritual flavour.

'If you read them carefully, sir,' I suddenly blurted out, 'you will find his writings not to be lacking in the flavour of Truth.' The fact is, rebellion had been long brewing within me. I was feeling done to death with mystic emotion. I was nauseated with shedding tears over abstract human feelings, to the neglect of living human creatures.

The Master blinked at me curiously before he replied: 'Very well, my son, carefully read them I will.' He tucked the books away under the bolster on which he reclined. I could perceive that his idea was not to surrender them to me.

Damini, from behind the door, must have got wind of this, for at once she stepped in and asked: 'Haven't the books you ordered for me arrived yet?'

I remained silent.

'My little mother!' said the Swami. 'These books are not fit for you to read.'

'How should you know that?'

The Master frowned. 'How, at least, could you know better?'

'I have read the author: you, perhaps, have not.'

'Why, then, need you read him over again?'

'When you have any need,' Damini flared up, 'nothing is allowed to stand in your way. It is only I who am to have no needs!'

'You forget yourself, Damini. I am a sannyasin. I have no worldly desires.'

'You forget that I am not a sannyasin. I have a desire to read these books. Will you kindly let me have them?'

The Swami drew out the books from under his bolster and tossed them across to me. I handed them over to Damini.

In the end, the books that Damini would have read alone by herself, she now began to send for me to read out to her. It was in that same shaded veranda along our rooms that these readings took place. Satish passed and repassed, longing to join in, but could not, unasked.

One day we had come upon a humorous passage, and Damini was rocking with laughter. There was a festival on at the temple and we had supposed that Satish would be there. But we heard a door open behind, through which Satish unexpectedly appeared and came and sat down beside us.

Damini's laughter was at once cut short. I also felt awkward. I wanted badly to say something to Satish, but no words would come, and I went on silently turning over page after page of my book. He rose, and left as abruptly as he had come. Our reading made no further progress that day.

Satish may very likely have understood that while he envied the absence of reserve between Damini and me, its presence was just what I envied in his case. That same day he petitioned the Master to be allowed to go off on a solitary excursion along the sea-coast, promising to be back within a week. 'The very thing, my son!' acquiesced the Swami, with enthusiasm.

Satish departed. Damini did not send for me to read to her any more, nor had she anything else to ask of me. Neither did I see her going to her friends, the women of the neighbourhood. She kept her room, with closed doors.

Some days passed thus. One afternoon, when the Master was deep in his siesta, and I was writing a letter seated out on our veranda, Satish suddenly turned up. Without so much as a glance at me, he walked straight up to Damini's door, knocking as he called: 'Damini, Damini.'

Damini came out at once. A strangely altered Satish met her inquiring gaze. Like a storm-battered ship, with torn rigging and tattered sails, was his condition, eyes wild, hair dishevelled, features drawn, garments dusty.

'Damini,' said Satish, 'I asked you to leave us. That was wrong of me. I beg your forgiveness.'

'Oh, don't say that,' cried the distressed Damini, clasping her hands.

'You must forgive me,' he repeated. 'I will never again allow that pride to overcome me, which led me to think I could take you or leave you, according to my own spiritual requirements. Such sin will never cross my mind again, I promise you. Do you also promise me one thing?' 'Command me!' said Damini, making humble obeisance.

'You must join us, and not keep aloof like this.'

'I will join you,' said Damini. 'I will sin no more.' Then, as she bowed low again to take the dust of his feet, she repeated, 'I will sin no more.'

V

The stone was melted again. Damini's bewildering radiance remained undimmed, but it lost its heat. In worship and ritual and service her beauty blossomed out anew. She was never absent from the kirtan singing, nor when the Master gave his readings and discourses. There was a change in her raiment also. She reverted to the golden brown of plain tussore, [Footnote: The tussore silk-worm is a wild variety, and its cocoon has to be used after the moth has cut its way out and flown away, thus not being killed in the process of unwinding the silk. Hence tussore silk is deemed specially suitable for wear on occasions of divine worship.] and whenever we saw her she seemed fresh from her toilet.

The severest test came in her intercourse with the Master. When she made her salutation to him, I could catch the glint of severely repressed temper through her half-closed eyelids. I knew very well that she could not bear to take orders from the Master; nevertheless, so complete was her self-suppression, that the Swami was able to screw up the courage to repeat his condemnation of the obnoxious tone of that outrageously modern Bengali writer. The next day there was a heap of flowers near his seat, and under them were the torn pages of the books of the objectionable author.

I had always noticed that the attendance on the Master by Satish was specially intolerable to Damini. Even now, when the Master asked him for some personal service, Damini would try to hustle past Satish and forestall him. This, however, was not possible in every case; and while Satish kept blowing on the tinder to get it into a blaze for the Master's pipe, Damini would have much ado to keep herself in hand by grimly repeating under her breath,'I will sin no more. I will sin no more.'

But what Satish had tried for did not come off. On the last occasion of Damini's self-surrender, he had seen the beauty of the surrender only, not of the self behind it. This time Damini herself had become so true for him that she eclipsed all strains of music, and all thoughts of philosophy. Her reality had become so dominant that Satish could no longer lose himself in his visions, nor think of her merely as an aspect of Universal Woman. It was not she who, as before, set off for him the melodies which filled his mind; rather, these melodies had now become part of the halo which encircled her person.

I should not, perhaps, leave out the minor detail that Damini had no longer any use for me. Her demands on me had suddenly ceased altogether. Of my colleagues, who used to assist in beguiling her leisure, the kite was dead, the mongoose had escaped, and as for the mongrel puppy, its manners having offended the Master's susceptibilities, it had been given away. Thus, bereft both of occupation and companionship, I returned to my old place in the assembly surrounding the Master, though the talking and singing and doing that went on there had all alike become horribly distasteful to me.

VI

The laboratory of Satish's mind was not amenable to any outside laws. One day, as he was compounding therein, for my special benefit, a weird mixture of ancient philosophy and modern science, with reason as well as emotion promiscuously thrown in, Damini burst in upon us, panting: 'Oh, do come, both of you, come quick!'

'Whatever is the matter?' I cried, as I leapt up.

'Nabin's wife has taken poison, I think,' she said.

Nabin was a neighbour, one of our regular kirtan singers, an ardent disciple. We hurried after Damini, but when we arrived his wife was dead.

We pieced together her story. Nabin's wife had brought her motherless younger sister to live with them. She was a very pretty girl, and when Nabin's brother had last been home, he was so taken with her that their marriage was speedily arranged. This greatly relieved her elder sister, for, high caste as they were, a suitable bridegroom was not easy to find. The wedding-day had been fixed some months later, when Nabin's brother would have completed his college course. Meanwhile Nabin's wife lit upon the discovery that her husband had seduced her sister. She forthwith insisted on his marrying the unfortunate girl, for which, as it happened, he did not require much persuasion. The wedding ceremony had just been put through, whereupon the elder sister had made away with herself by taking poison.

There was nothing to be done. The three of us slowly wended our way back, to find the usual throng round the Master. They sang a kirtan to him, and he waxed ecstatic in his usual manner, and began to dance with them.

That evening the moon was near its full. One corner of our terrace was overhung by the branch of a chalta tree. At the edge of the shadow, under its thick foliage, sat Damini lost in silent thought. Satish was softly pacing up and down our veranda behind her. I had a hobby for diary-writing, in which I was indulging, alone in my room, with the door wide open.

That evening the koil could not sleep; stirred by the south breeze the leaves too were speaking out, and the moonlight, shimmering on them, smiled in response. Something must also have stirred within Satish, for he suddenly turned his steps towards the terrace and went and stood near Damini.

Damini looked round with a start, adjusted her sari [Footnote: A formal recognition of the presence of an elder.] over the back of her head, and rose as if to leave. Satish called, 'Damini!'

She stopped at once, and turning to him appealingly with folded hands she said, 'My Master, may I ask you a question?'

Satish looked at her inquiringly, but made no reply.

Damini went on: 'Tell me truly, of what use to the world is this thing with which your sect is occupied day and night? Whom have you been able to save?'

I came out from my room and stood on the veranda.

Damini continued: 'This passion, passion, passion on which you harp, did you not see it in its true colours to-day? It has neither religion nor duty; it regards neither wife nor brother, nor the sanctuary of home; it knows neither pity nor trust, nor modesty, nor shame. What way have you discovered to save men from the hell of this cruel, shameless, soul-killing passion?'

I could not contain myself, but cried out: 'Oh yes, we have hit upon the wonderful device of banishing Woman right away from our territory, so as to make our pursuit of passion quite safe!'

Without paying any heed to my words, Damini spoke on to Satish: 'I have learnt nothing at all from your Master. He has never given me one moment's peace of mind. Fire cannot quench fire. The road along which he is taking his devotees leads neither to courage, nor restraint, nor peace. That poor woman who is dead, her heart's blood was sucked dry by this Fury, Passion, who killed her. Did you not see the hideous countenance of the murderess? For God's sake, my Master, I implore you, do not sacrifice me to that Fury. Oh, save me, for if anybody can save me, it is you!'

For a space all three of us kept silent. So poignant became the silence all around, it seemed to me that the vibrating drone of the cicadas was but a swoon-thrill of the pallid sky.

Satish was the first to speak. 'Tell me,' said he to Damini, 'what is it you would have me do for you?'

'Be my guru! I would follow none else. Give me some creed, higher than all this, which can save me. Do not let me be destroyed, together with the Divinity which is in me.'

Satish drew himself up straight, as he responded: 'So be it.'

Damini prostrated herself at his feet, her forehead touching the ground, and remained long thus, in reverential adoration, murmuring: 'Oh, my Master, my Master, save me, save me, save me from all sin.'

VII

Once more there was a mighty sensation in our world, and a storm of vituperation in the newspapers, for Satish had again turned renegade.

At first he had defiantly proclaimed active disbelief in all religion and social convention. Next, with equal vehemence, he had displayed active belief in gods and goddesses, rites and ceremonies, not excluding the least of them. Now, lastly, he had thrown to the winds all the rubbish-heaps both of religious and irreligious cults, and had retired into such simple peacefulness that no one could even guess what he believed, or what he did not. True, he took up good works as of old; but there was nothing aggressive about it this time.

There was another event over which the newspapers exhausted all their resources of sarcasm and virulence. That was the announcement of Damini's marriage with me. The mystery of this marriage none will perhaps fathom, but why need they?

CHAPTER IV

SRIVILAS

I

There was once an indigo factory on this spot. All that now remains of it are some tumble-down rooms belonging to the old house, the rest having crumbled into dust. When returning homewards, after performing Damini's last rites, the place, as we passed by it, somehow appealed to me, and I stayed on alone.

The road leading from the river-side to the factory gate is flanked by an avenue of sissoo trees. Two broken pillars still mark the site of the gateway, and portions of the garden wall are standing here and there. The only other memento of the past is the brick-built mound over the grave of some Mussulman servant of the factory. Through its cracks, wild flowering shrubs have sprung up. Covered with blossoms they sway to the breeze and mock at death, like merry maidens shaking with laughter while they chaff the bridegroom on his wedding-day. The banks of the garden pool have caved in and let the water trickle away, leaving the bottom to serve as a bed for a coriander patch. As I sit out on the roadside, under the shade of the avenue, the scent of the coriander, in flower, goes through and through my brain.

I sit and muse. The factory, of which these remnants are left, like the skeleton of some dead animal by the wayside, was once alive. From it flowed waves of pleasure and pain in a stormy succession, which then seemed to be endless. Its terribly efficient English proprietor, who made the very blood of his sweating cultivators run indigo-blue, how tremendous was he compared to puny me! Nevertheless, Mother Earth girded up her green mantle, undismayed, and set to work so thoroughly to plaster over the disfigurement wrought by him and his activities, that the few remaining traces require but a touch or two more to vanish for ever.

This scarcely novel reflection, however, was not what my mind ruminated over. 'No, no!' it protested. 'One dawn does not succeed another merely to smear fresh plaster [Footnote: The wattle-and-daub cottages of a Bengal village are cleaned and renovated every morning by a moist clay mixture being smeared by the housewife over the plinth and floors.] over the floor. True, the Englishman of the factory, together with the rest of its abominations, are all swept away into oblivion like a handful of dust, but my Damini!'

Many will not agree with me, I know. Shan-karacharya's philosophy spares no one. All the world is maya, a trembling dewdrop on the lotus leaf. But Shankaracharya was a sannyasin. 'Who is your wife, who your son?' were questions he asked, without understanding their meaning. Not being a sannyasin myself, I know full well that Damini is not a vanishing dewdrop on the lotus leaf.

But, I am told, there are householders also, who say the same thing. That may be. They are mere householders, who have lost only the mistress of their house. Their home is doubtless maya, and so likewise is its mistress. These are their own handiwork, and when done with any broom is good enough for sweeping their fragments clean away.

I did not keep house long enough to settle down as a householder, nor is mine the temperament of a sannyasin, that saved me. So the Damini whom I gained became neither housewife nor maya. She ever remained true to herself, my Damini. Who dares to call her a shadow?

Had I known Damini only as mistress of my house, much of this would never have been written. It is because I knew her in a greater, truer relation, that I have no hesitation in putting down the whole truth, recking nothing of what others may say.

Had it been my lot to live with Damini, as others do in the everyday world, the household routine of toilet and food and repose would have sufficed for me as for them. And after Damini's death, I could have heaved a sigh and exclaimed with Shankaracharya: 'Variegated is the world of maya!' before hastening to honour the suggestion of some aunt, or other well-meaning elder, by another attempt to sample its variety by marrying again. But I had not adjusted myself to the domestic world, like a foot in a comfortable old shoe. From the very outset I had given up hope of happiness, no, no, that is saying too much; I was not so non-human as that. Happiness I certainly hoped for, but I did not arrogate to myself the right to claim it.

Why? Because it was I who persuaded Damini to give her consent to our marriage. Not for us was the first auspicious vision [Footnote: At one stage of the wedding ceremony a red screen is placed round the Bride and Bridegroom, and they are asked to look at each other. This is the Auspicious Vision,] in the rosy glow of festive lamps, to the rapturous strains of wedding pipes. We married in the broad light of day, with eyes wide open.

II

When we went away from Lilananda Swami, the time came to think of ways and means, as well as of a sheltering roof. We had all along been more in danger of surfeit than of starvation, with the hospitality which the devotees of the Master pressed on us, wherever we went with him. We had almost come to forget that to be a householder involves the acquiring, or building, or at least the renting of a house, so accustomed had we become to cast the burden of its supply upon another, and to look on a house as demanding from us only the duty of making ourselves thoroughly comfortable in it.

At length we recollected that Uncle Jagamohan had bequeathed his share of the house to Satish. Had the will been left in Satish's custody, it would by this time have been wrecked, like a paper boat, on the waves of his emotion. It happened, however, to be with me; for I was the executor. There were three conditions attached to the bequest which I was responsible for carrying out. No religious worship was to be performed in the house. The ground floor was to be used as a school for the leather-dealers' children. And after Satish's death, the whole property was to be applied for the benefit of that community. Piety was the one thing Uncle Jagamohan could not tolerate. He looked on it as more defiling even than worldliness; and probably these provisions, which he facetiously referred to in English as 'sanitary precautions,' were intended as a safeguard against the excessive piety which prevailed in the adjoining half of the house.

'Come along,' I said to Satish. 'Let's go to your Calcutta house.'

'I am not quite ready for that yet,' Satish replied.

I did not understand him.

'There was a day,' he explained, 'when I relied wholly on reason, only to find at last that reason could not support the whole of life's burden. There was another day, when I placed my reliance on emotion, only to discover it to be a bottomless abyss. The reason and the emotion, you see, were alike mine. Man cannot rely on himself alone. I dare not return to town until I have found my support.'

'What then do you suggest?' I asked.

'You two go on to the Calcutta house. I would wander alone for a time. I seem to see glimpses of the shore. If I allow it out of my sight now, I may lose it forever.'

As soon as we were by ourselves, Damini said to me: 'That will never do! If he wanders about alone, who is to look after him? Don't you remember in what plight he came back when he last went wandering? The very idea of it fills me with fear.'

Shall I tell the truth? This anxiety of Damini's stung me like a hornet, leaving behind the smart of anger. Had not Satish wandered about for two whole years after Uncle Jagamohan's death, had that killed him? My question did not remain unuttered. Rather, some of the smart of the sting got expressed with it.

'I know, Srivilas Babu,' Damini replied. 'It takes a great deal to kill a man. But why should he be allowed to suffer at all, so long as the two of us are here to prevent it?'

The two of us! Half of that meant this wretched creature, Srivilas! It is of course a law of the world, that in order to save some people from suffering others shall suffer. All the inhabitants of the earth may be divided into two such classes. Damini had found out to which I belonged. It was compensation, indeed, that she included herself in the same class.

I went and said to Satish: 'All right, then, let us postpone our departure to town. We can stay for a time in that dilapidated house on the river-side. They say it is subject to ghostly visitations. This will serve to keep off human visitors.'

'And you two?' inquired Satish.

'Like the ghosts, we shall keep in hiding as far as possible.'

Satish threw a nervous glance at Damini, there may have been a suggestion of dread in it.

Damini clasped her hands as she said imploringly: 'I have accepted you as my guru.

Whatever my sins may have been, let them not deprive me of the right to serve you.'

III

I must confess that this frenzied pertinacity of Satish's quest is beyond my understanding. There was a time when I would have laughed to scorn the very idea. Now I had ceased to laugh. What Satish was pursuing was fire indeed, no will-o'-the-wisp. When I realised how its heat was consuming him, the old arguments of Uncle Jagamohan's school refused to pass my lips. Of what avail would it be to find, with Herbert Spencer, that the mystic sense might have originated in some ghostly superstition, or that its message could be reduced to some logical absurdity? Did we not see how Satish was burning, his whole being aglow?

Satish was perhaps better off when his days were passing in one round of excitement, singing, dancing, serving the Master, the whole of his spiritual effort exhausting itself in the output of the moment. Since he has lapsed into outward quiet, his spirit refuses to be controlled any longer. There is now no question of seeking emotional satisfaction. The inward struggle for realisation is so tremendous within him, that we are afraid to look on his face.

I could remain silent no longer. 'Satish,' I suggested,'don't you think it would be better to go to some guru who could show you the way and make your spiritual progress easier?'

This only served to annoy him. 'Oh, do be quiet, Visri,' he broke out irritably. 'For goodness' sake keep quiet! What does one want to make it easier for? Delusion alone is easy. Truth is always difficult.'

'But would it not be better,' I tried again, 'if some guru were to guide you along the path of Truth?'

Satish was almost beside himself. 'Will you never understand,' he groaned,'that I am not running after any geographical truth? The Dweller within can only come to me along my own true path. The path of the guru can only lead to the guru's door.'

What a number of opposite principles have I heard enunciated by this same mouth of Satish! I, Srivilas, once the favourite disciple of Uncle Jagamohan, who would have threatened me with a big stick if I had called him Master, had actually been made by Satish to massage the legs of Lila-nanda Swami. And now not even a week has passed but he needs must preach to me in this strain! However, as I dared not smile, I maintained a solemn silence.

'I have now understood,' Satish went on, 'why our Scriptures say that it is better to die in one's own dharma rather than court the terrible fate of taking the dharma of another. All else may be accepted as gifts, but if one's dharma is not one's own, it does not save, but kills. I cannot gain my God as alms from anybody else. If I get Him at all, it shall be I who win Him. If I do not, even death is better.'

I am argumentative by nature, and could not give in so easily. 'A poet,' said I,'may get a poem from within himself. But he who is not a poet needs must take it from another.'

'I am a poet,' said Satish, without blenching.

That finished the matter. I came away.

Satish had no regular hours for meals or sleep. There was no knowing where he was to be found next. His body began to take on the unsubstantial keenness of an over sharpened knife. One felt this could not go on much longer. Yet I could not muster up courage to interfere. Damini, however, was utterly unable to bear it. She was grievously incensed at God's ways. With those who ignored Him, God was powerless, was it fair thus to take it out of one who was helplessly prostrate at His feet? When Damini used to wax wroth with Lilananda Swami, she knew how to bring it home to him. Alas, she knew not how to bring her feelings home to God! Anyhow, she spared no pains in trying to get Satish to be regular in satisfying his physical needs. Numberless and ingenious were her contrivances to get this misfit creature to conform to domestic regulations. For a considerable space Satish made no overt objection to her endeavours. But one morning he waded across the shallow river to the broad sand-bed along the opposite bank, and there disappeared from sight.

The sun rose to the meridian; it gradually bent over to the west; but there was no sign of Satish. Damini waited for him, fasting, till she could contain herself no longer. She put some food on a salver, and with it toiled through the knee-deep water, and at last found herself on the sand-bank.

It was a vast expanse on which not a living creature of any kind was to be seen. The sun was cruel. Still more so were the glowing billows of sand, one succeeding the other, like ranks of crouching sentinels guarding the emptiness. As she stood on the edge of this spreading pallor, where all limits seemed to have been lost, where no call could meet with any response, no question with any answer, Damini's heart sank within her. It was as if her world had been wiped away and reduced to the dull blank of original colourlessness. One vast 'No' seemed to be stretched at her feet. No sound, no movement, no red of blood, no green of vegetation, no blue of sky, but only the drab of sand. It looked like the lipless grin of some giant skull, the tongueless cavern of its jaws gaping with an eternal petition of thirst to the unrelenting fiery skies above.

While she was wondering in what direction to proceed, the faint track of footsteps caught Damini's eye. These she pursued, and went on and on, over the undulating surface, till they stopped at a pool on the farther side of a sand-drift. Along the moist edge of the water could be seen the delicate tracery of the claw-marks of innumerable water-fowl. Under the shade of the sand-drift sat Satish.

The water was the deepest of deep blue. The fussy snipe were poking about on its margin, bobbing their tails and fluttering their black-and-white wings. At some distance were a flock of wild duck quacking vigorously, and seeming never to get the preening of their feathers done to their own satisfaction. When Damini reached the top of the mound, which formed one bank of the pool, the ducks took themselves off in a body, with a great clamour and beating of wings. Satish looked round and saw Damini. 'Why are you here?' he cried.

'I have brought you something to eat,' said Damini.

'I want nothing,' said Satish.

'It is very late -' ventured Damini.

'Nothing at all,' repeated Satish.

'Let me then wait a little,' suggested Damini. 'Perhaps later on -?'

'Oh, why will you-' burst out Satish, but as his glance fell on Damini's face he stopped short.

Damini said nothing further. Tray in hand she retraced her steps through the sand, which glared round her like the eye of a tiger in the dark.

Tears had always been rarer in Damini's eyes than lightning flashes. But when I saw her that evening, seated on the floor, her feet stretched out before her, she was weeping. When she saw me her tears seemed to burst through some obstruction and showered forth in torrents. I cannot tell what it felt like within my breast. I came near and sat down on one side.

When she had calmed herself a little I inquired: 'Why does Satish's health make you so anxious?'

'What else have I to be anxious about?' she asked simply. 'All the rest he has to think out for himself. There I can neither understand nor help.'

'But consider, Damini,' I said. 'When man's mind puts forth all its energy into one particular channel, his bodily needs become reduced correspondingly. That is why, in the presence of great joy or great sorrow, man does not hunger or thirst. Satish's state of mind is now such that it will do him no harm even if you do not look after his body.'

'I am a woman,' replied Damini. 'The building up of the body with our own body, with our life itself, is our dharma. It is woman's own creation. So when we women see the body suffer, our spirit refuses to be comforted.'

'That is why,' I retorted,'those who are busy with things of the spirit seem to have no eyes for you, the guardians of mere bodies!'

'Haven't they!' Damini flared up. 'So wonderful, rather, is the vision of their eyes, it turns everything topsy-turvy.'

'Ah, woman,' said I to myself. 'That is what fascinates you. Srivilas, my boy, next time you take birth, take good care to be born in the world of topsy-turvydom.'

IV

The wound which Satish inflicted on Damini that day on the sands had this result, that he could not remove from his mind the agony he had seen in her eyes. During the succeeding days he had to go through the purgatory of showing her special consideration. It was long since he had freely conversed with us. Now he would send for Damini and talk to her. The experiences and struggles through which he was passing were the subject of these talks.

Damini had never been so exercised by his indifference as she now was by his solicitude. She felt sure this could not last, because the cost was too much to pay. Some day or other Satish's attention would be drawn to the state of the account, and he would discover how high the price was; then would come the crash. The more regular Satish became in his meals and rest, as a good householder should, the more anxious became Damini, the more she felt ashamed of herself. It was almost as if she would be relieved to find Satish becoming rebellious. She seemed to be saying: 'You were quite right to hold aloof. Your concern for me is only punishing yourself. That I cannot bear! I must,' she appeared to conclude,'make friends with the neighbours again, and see if I cannot contrive to keep away from the house.'

One night we were roused by a sudden shout: 'Srivilas! Damini!' It must have been past midnight, but Satish could not have taken count of the hour. How he passed his nights we knew not, but the way he went on seemed to have cowed the very ghosts into flight.

We shook off our slumbers, and came out of our respective rooms to find Satish on the flagged pavement in front of the house, standing alone in the darkness. 'I have understood!' he exclaimed as he saw us. 'I have no more doubts.'

Damini softly went up and sat down on the pavement. Satish absently followed her example and sat down too. I also followed suit.

'If I keep going,' said Satish, 'in the same direction along which He comes to me, then I shall only be going further and further away from Him. If I proceed in the opposite direction, then only can we meet.'

I silently gazed at his flaming eyes. As a geometrical truth what he said was right enough. But what in the world was it all about? 'He loves form,' Satish went on, 'so He is continually descending towards form. We cannot live by form alone, so we must ascend towards His formlessness. He is free, so His play is within bonds. We are bound, so we find our joy in freedom. All our sorrow is because we cannot understand this.'

We kept as silent as the stars.

'Do you not understand, Damini?' pursued Satish. 'He who sings proceeds from his joy to the tune; he who hears, from the tune to joy. One comes from freedom into bondage, the other goes from bondage into freedom; only thus can they have their communion. He sings and we hear. He ties the bonds as He sings to us, we untie them as we hear Him.'

I cannot say whether Damini understood Satish's words, but she understood Satish. With her hands folded on her lap she kept quite still.

'I was hearing His song through the night,' Satish went on, 'till in a flash the whole thing became clear to me. Then I could not keep it to myself, and called out to you. All this time I had been trying to fashion Him to suit myself, and so was deprived. O Desolator! Breaker of ties! Let me be shattered to pieces within you, again and again, forever and ever. Bonds are not for me, that is why I cannot hold on to bonds for long. Bonds are yours, and so are you kept eternally bound to creation. Play on, then, with our forms and let me take my flight into your formlessness. O Eternal, you are mine, mine, mine!' Satish departed into the night towards the river.

After that night, Satish lapsed back into his old ways, forgetful of all claims of rest or nourishment. As to when his mind would rise into the light of ecstasy, or lapse into the depths of gloom, we could make no guess. May God help her who has taken on herself the burden of keeping such a creature within the wholesomeness of worldly habit....

V

It had been stiflingly oppressive the whole day. In the night a great storm burst on us. We had our several rooms along a veranda, in which a light used to be kept burning all night. That was now blown out. The river was lashed into foaming waves, and a flood of rain burst forth from the clouds. The splashing of the waves down below, and the dashing of the torrents from above, played the cymbals in this chaotic revel of the gods. Nothing could be seen of the deafening movements which resounded within the depths of the darkness, and made the sky, like a blind child, break into shivers of fright. Out of the bamboo thickets pierced a scream as of some bereaved giantess. From the mango groves burst the cracking and crashing of breaking timber. The river, side echoed with the deep thuds of falling masses from the crumbling banks. Through the bare ribs of our dilapidated house the keen blasts howled and howled like infuriated beasts.

On such a night the fastenings of the human mind are shaken loose. The storm gains entry and plays havoc within, scattering into disorder its well-arranged furniture of convention, tossing about its curtains of decorous restraint in disturbing revealment. I could not sleep. But what can I write of the thoughts which assailed my sleepless brain? They do not concern this story.

'Who is that?' I heard Satish cry out all of a sudden in the darkness.

'It is I, Damini,' came the reply. 'Your windows are open, and the rain is streaming in. I have come to close them.'

As she was doing this, she found Satish had got out of his bed. He seemed to stand and hesitate, just for a moment, and then he went out of the room.

Damini went back to her own room and sat long on the threshold. No one returned. The fury of the wind went on increasing in violence.

Damini could sit quiet no longer. She also left the house. It was hardly possible to keep on one's feet in the storm. The sentinels of the revelling gods seemed to be scolding Damini and repeatedly thrusting her back. The rain made desperate attempts to pervade every nook and cranny of the sky.

A flash rent the sky from end to end with terrific tearing thunder. It revealed Satish standing on the river brink. With a supreme effort Damini reached him in one tempestuous rush, outvying the wind. She fell prone at his feet. The shriek of the storm was overcome by her cry: 'At your feet, I swear I had no thought of sin against your God! Why punish me thus?' Satish stood silent.

'Thrust me into the river with your feet, if you would be rid of me. But return you must!'

Satish came back. As he re-entered the house he said: 'My need for Him whom I seek is immense, so absolutely, that I have no need for anything else at all. Damini, have pity on me and leave me to Him.'

After a space of silence Damini said: 'I will.'

VI

I knew nothing of this at the time, but heard it all from Damini afterwards. So when I saw through my open door the two returning figures pass along the veranda to their rooms, the desolation of my lot fell heavy on my heart and took me by the throat. I struggled up from my bed. Further sleep was impossible that night.

Next morning, what a changed Damini met my eyes! The demon dance of last night's storm seemed to have left all its ravages on this one forlorn girl. Though I knew nothing of what had happened, I felt bitterly angry with Satish.

'Srivilas Babu,' said Damini, 'will you take me on to Calcutta?'

I could guess all that these words meant for her; so I asked no question. But, in the midst of the torture within me, I felt the balm of consolation. It was well that Damini should take herself away from here. Repeated buffeting against the rock could only end in the vessel being broken up.

At parting, Damini made her obeisance to Satish, saying: 'I have grievously sinned at your feet. May I hope for pardon?'

Satish, with his eyes fixed on the ground, replied: 'I also have sinned. Let me first purge my sin away, and then will I claim forgiveness.'

It became clear to me, on our way to Calcutta, what a devastating fire had all along been raging within Damini. I was so scorched by its heat that I could not restrain myself from breaking out in revilement of Satish.

Damini stopped me frenziedly. 'Don't you dare talk so in my presence!' she exclaimed. 'Little do you know what he saved me from! You can only see my sorrow. Had you no eyes for the sorrow he has been through, in order to save me? The hideous tried once to destroy the beautiful, and got well kicked for its pains. Serve it right! Serve it right!' Damini began to beat her breast violently with her clenched hands. I had to hold them back by main force.

When we arrived in the evening, I left Damini at her aunt's and went over to a lodging-house, where I used to be well known. My old acquaintances started at sight of me. 'Have you been ill?' they cried.

By next morning's post I got a letter from Damini. 'Take me away,' she wrote. 'There is no room for me here.'

It appeared that her aunt would not have her. Scandal about us was all over the town. The Pooja numbers of the weekly newspapers had come out shortly after we had given up Lilananda Swami. All the instruments for our execution had been kept sharpened. The carnage turned out to be worthy of the occasion. In our shastras the sacrifice of she-animals is prohibited. But, in the case of modern human sacrifice, a woman victim seems to add to the zest of the performers. The mention of Damini's name was skilfully avoided. But no less was the skill which did away with all doubt as to the intention. Anyhow, it had resulted in this shrinkage of room in the house of Damini's distant aunt.

Damini had lost her parents. But I had an idea that her brother was living. I asked Damini for his address, but she shook her head, saying they were too poor. The fact was, Damini did not care to place her brother in an awkward position. What if he also came to say there was no room?

'Where will you stay, then?' I had to inquire.

'I will go back to Lilananda Swami.' I could not trust myself to speak for a time, I was so overcome. Was this, then, the last cruel trick which Fate had held in reserve?

'Will the Swami take you back?' I asked at length.

'Gladly!'

Damini understood men. Sect-mongers rejoice more in capturing adherents than in comprehending truths. Damini was quite right. There would be no dearth of room for her at Lilananda's, but -

'Damini,' I said, just at this juncture. 'There is another way. If you promise not to be angry, I will mention it.'

'Tell me,' said Damini.

'If it is at all possible for you to think of marrying a creature, such as I am -'

'What are you saying, Srivilas Babu?' interrupted Damini. 'Are you mad?'

'Suppose I am,' said I. 'One can sometimes solve insoluble problems by becoming mad. Madness is like the wishing carpet of the Arabian Nights. It can waft one over the thousand petty considerations which obstruct the everyday world.'

'What do you call petty considerations?'

'Such as: What will people think? What will happen in the future? and so on, and so forth.'

'And what about the vital considerations?'

'What do you call vital?' I asked in my turn.

'Such as, for instance: What will be your fate if you marry a creature like me?' said Damini.

'If that be a vital consideration, I am reassured. For I cannot possibly be in a worse plight than now. Any movement of my prostrate fortune, even though it be a turning over to the other side, cannot but be a sign of improvement.'

Of course I could not believe that some telepathic news of my state of mind had never reached Damini. Such news, however, had not, so far, come under the head of 'Important' at least it had not called for any notice to be taken. Now action was definitely demanded of her.

Damini was lost in silent thought.

'Damini,' I said, 'I am only one of the very ordinary sort of men, even less, for I am of no account in the world. To marry me, or not to marry me, cannot make enough difference to be worth all this thought.'

Tears glistened in Damini's eyes. 'Had you been an ordinary man, it would not have cost me a moment's hesitation,' she said.

After another long silence, Damini murmured: 'You know what I am.'

'You also know what I am,' I rejoined.

Thus was the proposal mooted, relying more on things unspoken than on what was said.

VII

Those who, in the old days, had been under the spell of my English speeches had mostly shaken off their fascination during my absence; except only Naren, who still looked on me as one of the rarest products of the age. A house belonging to him was temporarily vacant. In this we took shelter.

It seemed at first that my proposal would never be rescued from the ditch of silence, into which it had lumbered at the very start; or at all events that it would require any amount of discussion and repair work before it could be hauled back on the high road of 'yes' or 'no.'

But man's mind was evidently created to raise a laugh against mental science, with its sudden practical jokes. In the spring, which now came upon us, the Creator's joyous laughter rang through and through this hired dwelling of ours.

All this while Damini never had the time to notice that I was anybody at all; or it may be that the dazzling light from a different quarter had kept her blinded. Now that her world had shrunk around her, it was reduced to me alone. So she had no help but to look on me with seeing eyes. Perhaps it was the kindness of my fate which contrived that this should be her first sight of me.

By river and hill and seashore have I wandered along with Damini, as one of Lilananda's kirtan party, setting the atmosphere on fire with passionate song, to the beat of drum and cymbal. Great sparks of emotion were set free as we rang the changes on the text of the Vaishanava poet: The noose of love hath bound my heart to thy feet. Yet the curtain which hid me from Damini was not burnt away.

But what was it that happened in this Calcutta lane? The dingy houses, crowding upon one another, blossomed out like flowers of paradise. Verily God vouchsafed to us a miracle. Out of this brick and mortar He fashioned a harp-string to voice forth His melody. And with His wand He touched me, the least of men, and made me, all in a moment, wonderful.

When the curtain is there, the separation is infinite; when it is lifted, the distance can be crossed in the twinkling of an eye. So it took no time at all. 'I was in a dream,' said Damini. 'It wanted this shock to wake me. Between that "you" of mine and this "you" of mine, there was a veil of stupor. I salute my Master again and again, for it is he who dispelled it.'

'Damini,' I said,'do not keep your gaze on me like that. Before, when you made the discovery that this creation of God is not beautiful, I was able to bear it; but it will be difficult to do so now.'

'I am making the discovery,' she replied,'that this creation of God has its beauty.'

'Your name will go down in history!' I exclaimed. 'The planting of the explorer's flag on the South Pole heights was child's play to this discovery of yours. "Difficult" is not the word for it. You will have achieved the impossible!'

I had never realised before how short our spring month of Phalgun is. It has only thirty days, and each of the days is not a minute more than twenty-four hours. With the infinite time which God has at His disposal, such parsimony I failed to understand!

'This mad freak that you are bent on,' said Damini; 'what will your people have to say to it?'

'My people are my best friends. So they are sure to turn me out of their house.'

'What next?'

'Next it will be for you and me to build up a home, fresh from the very foundations, that will be our own special creation.'

'You must also fashion afresh the mistress of your house, from the very beginning. May she also be your creation, with no trace left of her old battered condition!'

We fixed a day in the following month for the wedding. Damini insisted that Satish should be brought over.

'What for?' I asked.

'He must give me away.'

Where the madcap was wandering I was not sure. I had written several letters, but with no reply. He could hardly have given up that old haunted house, otherwise my letters would have been returned as undelivered. The chances were that he had not the time to be opening and reading letters.

'Damini,' said I, 'you must come with me and invite him personally. This is not a case for sending a formal invitation letter. I could have gone by myself, but my courage is not equal to it. For all we know, he may be on the other side of the river, superintending the preening of ducks' feathers. To follow him there is a desperate venture of which you alone are capable!'

Damini smiled. 'Did I not swear I would never pursue him there again?'

'You swore you would not go to him with food any more. That does not cover your going over to invite him to a repast!'

VIII

This time everything passed off smoothly. We each took Satish by one hand and brought him along with us back to Calcutta. He was as pleased as a child receiving a pair of new dolls!

Our idea had been to have a quiet wedding. But Satish would have none of that. Moreover, there were the Mussulman friends of Uncle Jagamohan. When they heard the news, they were so extravagantly jubilant that the neighbours must have thought it was for the Amir of Kabul or the Nizam of Hyderabad, at the very least. But the height of revelry was reached by the newspapers in a very orgy of calumny. Our hearts, however, were too full to harbour any resentment. We were quite willing to allow the blood-thirstiness of the readers to be satisfied, and the pockets of the proprietors to be filled, along with our blessings to boot.

'Come and occupy my house, Visri, old fellow,' said Satish.

'Come with us, too,' I added. 'Let us set to work together over again.'

'No, thank you,' said Satish. 'My work is elsewhere.'

'You won't be allowed to go till you have assisted at our house-warming,' insisted Damini.

This function was not going to be a crowded affair, Satish being the only guest. But it was all very well for him to say: 'Come and occupy my house.' That had already been done by his father, Harimohan, not directly, but through a tenant. Harimohan would have entered into possession himself, but his worldly and other-worldly advisers warned him that it was best not to risk it, a Mussulman having died there of the plague. Of course the tenant to whom it was offered ran the same spiritual and physical risks, but then why need he be told?

How we got the house out of Harimohan's clutches is a long story. The Mussulman leather-dealers were our chief allies. When they got to know the contents of the will, we found further legal steps to be superfluous.

The allowance which I had all along been getting from home was now stopped. It was all the more of a joy to us to undertake together the toil of setting up house without outside assistance. With the seal of Premchand-Roychand it was not difficult for me to secure a professorship. I was able to supplement my income by publishing notes on the prescribed text books, which were eagerly availed of as patent nostrums for passing examinations. I need not have done so much, for our own wants were few. But Damini insisted that Satish should not have to worry about his own living while we were here to prevent it.

There was another thing about which Damini did not say a word. I had to attend to it secretly. That was the education of her brother's son and the marriage of his daughter. Both of these matters were beyond the means of her brother himself. His house was barred to us, but pecuniary assistance has no caste to stand in the way of its acceptance. Moreover, acceptance did not necessarily involve acknowledgment. So I had to add the sub-editorship of a newspaper to my other occupations.

Without consulting Damini, I engaged a cook and two servants. Without consulting me, Damini sent them packing the very next day. When I objected, she made me conscious how ill-judged was my attempted consideration for her. 'If I am not allowed,' she said, 'to do my share of work while you are slaving away, where am I to hide my shame?'

My work outside and Damini's work at home flowed on together like the confluent Ganges and Jumna. Damini also began to teach sewing to the leather-dealers' little girls. She was determined not to take defeat at my hands. I am not enough of a poet to sing how this Calcutta house of ours became Brindaban itself, our labours the flute strains which kept it enraptured. All I can say is that our days did not drag, neither did they merely pass by, they positively danced along.

One more springtime came and went; but never another.

Ever since her return from the cave-temple Damini had suffered from a pain in her breast, of which, however, she then told no one. This suddenly took a turn for the worse, and when I asked her about it she said: 'This is my secret wealth, my touchstone. With it, as dower, I was able to come to you. Otherwise I would not have been worthy.'

The doctors, each of them, had a different name for the malady. Neither did they agree in their prescriptions. When my little hoard of gold was blown away between the cross-fire of the doctors' fees and the chemist's bills, the chapter of medicament came to an end, and change of air was advised. As a matter of fact, hardly anything of changeable value was left to us except air.

'Take me to the place from which I brought the pain,' said Damini. 'It has no dearth of air.'

When the month of Magh ended with its full moon and Phalgun began, while the sea heaved and sobbed with the wail of its lonely eternity, Damini, taking the dust of my feet, bade farewell to me with the words:

'I have not had enough of you. May you be mine again in our next birth.'

IN THE NIGHT

'Doctor, Doctor!'

I was startled out of my sleep in the very depth of night. On opening my eyes I saw it was our landlord Dokhin Babu. Hurriedly getting up and drawing out a broken chair, I made him sit down, and looked anxiously in his face. I saw by the clock that it was after half-past two.

Dokhin Babu's face was pale, and his eyes wide open, as he said: 'To-night those symptoms returned that medicine of yours has done me no good at all.' I said rather timidly: 'I am afraid you have been drinking again.' Dokhin Babu got quite angry, and said: 'There you make a great mistake. It is not the drink. You must hear the whole story in order to be able to understand the real reason.'

In the niche there was a small tin kerosene lamp burning dimly. This I turned up slightly; the light became a little brighter, and at the same time it began to smoke. Pulling my cloth over my shoulders, I spread a piece of newspaper over a packing-case, and sat down. Dokhin Babu began his story:

'About four years ago I was attacked by a serious illness; just when I was on the point of death my disease took a better turn, until, after nearly a month, I recovered.

'During my illness my wife did not rest for a moment, day or night. For those months that weak woman fought with all her might to drive Death's messenger from the door. She went without food and sleep, and had no thought for anything else in this world.

'Death, like a tiger cheated of its prey, threw me from its jaws, and went off, but in its retreat it dealt my wife a sharp blow with its paw.

'Not long after my wife gave birth to a dead child. Then came my turn to nurse her. But she got quite troubled at this, and would say: "For heaven's sake, don't keep fussing in and out of my room like that."

'If I went to her room at night when she had fever, and, on the pretence of fanning myself, would try to fan her, she would get quite excited. And if, on account of serving her, my meal-time was ten minutes later than usual, that also was made the occasion for all sorts of entreaties and reproaches. If I went to do her the smallest service, instead of helping her it had just the opposite effect. She would exclaim: "It's not good for a man to fuss so much."

'I think you have seen my garden-house. In front of it is the garden, at the foot of which the river Ganges flows. Towards the south, just below our bedroom, my wife had made a garden according to her own fancy, and surrounded it with a hedge of henna. It was the one bit of the garden that was simple and unpretentious. In the flower-pots you did not see wooden pegs with long Latin names flying pretentious flags by the side of the most unpretentious-looking plants. Jasmine, tuberose, lemon flowers, and all kinds of roses were plentiful. Under a large bokul tree there was a white marble slab, which my wife used to wash twice a day when she was in good health. It was the place where she was in the habit of sitting on summer evenings, when her work was finished. From there she could see the river, but was herself invisible to the travellers on the passing steamers.

'One moonlight evening in the month of April, after having been confined to her bed for many days, she expressed a desire to get out of her close room, and sit in her garden.

'I lifted her with great care, and laid her down on that marble seat under the bokul tree. One or two bokul flowers fluttered down, and through the branches overhead the chequered moonlight fell on her worn face. All around was still and silent. As I looked down on her face, sitting by her side in that shadowy darkness, filled with the heavy scent of flowers, my eyes became moist.

'Slowly drawing near her, I took one of her hot thin hands between my own. She made no attempt to prevent me. After I had sat like this in silence for some time, my heart began to overflow, and I said: "Never shall I be able to forget your love."

'My wife gave a laugh in which there were mingled some happiness, a trace of distrust, and also the sharpness of sarcasm. She said nothing in the way of an answer, and yet gave me to understand by her laugh that she thought it unlikely that I would never forget her, nor did she herself wish it.

'I had never had the courage to make love to my wife simply out of fear of this sweet sharp laugh of hers. All the speeches which I made up when I was absent from her seemed to be very commonplace as soon as I found myself in her presence.

'It is possible to talk when you are contradicted, but laughter cannot be met by argument; so I had simply to remain silent. The moonlight became brighter, and a cuckoo began to call over and over again till it seemed to be demented. As I sat still, I wondered how on such a night the cuckoo's bride could remain indifferent.

'After a great deal of treatment, my wife's illness showed no signs of improvement. The doctor suggested a change of air, and I took her to Allahabad.'

At this point Dokhin Babu suddenly stopped, and sat silent. With a questioning look on his face he looked towards me, and then began to brood with his head resting in his hands. I too kept silence. The kerosene lamp flickered in the niche, and in the stillness of the night the buzzing of the mosquitoes could be heard distinctly. Suddenly breaking the silence, Dokhin Babu resumed his story:

'Doctor Haran treated my wife, and after some time I was told that the disease was an incurable one, and my wife would have to suffer for the rest of her life.

'Then one day my wife said to me: "Since my disease is not going to leave me, and there does not seem much hope of my dying soon, why should you spend your days with this living death? Leave me alone, and go back to your other occupations."

'Now it was my turn to laugh. But I had not got her power of laughter. So, with all the solemnity suitable to the hero of a romance, I asserted: "So long as there is life in this body of mine -"

'She stopped me, saying: "Now, now. You don't need to say any more. Why, to hear you makes me want to give up the ghost."

'I don't know whether I had actually confessed it to myself then, but now I know quite well that I had, even at that time, in my heart of hearts, got tired of nursing the hopeless invalid.

'It was clear that she was able to detect my inner weariness of spirit, in spite of my devoted service. I did not understand it then, but now I have not the least doubt in my mind that she could read me as easily as a Children's First Reader in which there are no compound letters.

'Doctor Haran was of the same caste as myself. I had a standing invitation to his house. After I had been there several times he introduced me to his daughter. She was unmarried, although she was over fifteen years old. Her father said that he had not married her as he had not been able to find a suitable bridegroom of the same caste, but rumour said that there was some bar sinister in her birth.

'But she had no other fault, for she was as intelligent as she was beautiful. For that reason I used sometimes to discuss with her all sorts of questions, so that it was often late at night before I got back home, long past the time when I should have given my wife her medicine. She knew quite well that I had been at Doctor Haran's house, but she never once asked me the cause of my delay.

'The sick-room seemed to me doubly intolerable and joyless. I now began to neglect my patient, and constantly forgot to give her the medicine at the proper time.

'The doctor used sometimes to say to me: "For those who suffer from some incurable disease death would be a happy release. As long as they remain alive they get no happiness themselves, and make others miserable."

'To say this in the ordinary course might be tolerated, but, with the example of my wife before us, such a subject ought not to have been mentioned. But I suppose doctors grow callous about the question of life and death of men.

'Suddenly one day, as I was sitting in the room next to the sick chamber, I heard my wife say to the doctor: "Doctor, why do you go on giving me so many useless medicines? When my whole life has become one continuous disease, don't you think that to kill me is to cure me?"

'The doctor said: "You shouldn't talk like that."

'As soon as the doctor had gone, I went into my wife's room, and seating myself beside her began to stroke her forehead gently. She said: "This room is very hot, you go out for your usual walk. If you don't get your evening exercise, you will have no appetite for your dinner."

'My evening walk meant going to Doctor Haran's house. I had myself explained that a little exercise is necessary for one's health and appetite. Now I am quite sure that every day she saw through my excuse. I was the fool, and I actually thought that she was unconscious of this deception.'

Here Dokhin Babu paused and, burying his head in his hands, remained silent for a time. At last he said: 'Give me a glass of water,' and having drunk the water he continued:

'One day the doctor's daughter Monorama expressed a desire to see my wife. I don't quite know why, but this proposal did not altogether please me. But I could find no excuse for refusing her request. So she arrived one evening at our house.

'On that day my wife's pain had been rather more severe than usual. When her pain was worse she would lie quite still and silent, occasionally clenching her fists. It was only from that one was able to guess what agony she was enduring. There was no sound in the room, and I was sitting silently at the bedside. She had not requested me to go out for my usual walk. Either she had not the power to speak, or she got some relief from having me by her side when she was suffering very much. The kerosene lamp had been placed near the door lest it should hurt her eyes. The room was dark and still. The only sound that could be heard was an occasional sigh of relief when my wife's pain became less for a moment or two.

'It was at this time that Monorama came, and stood at the door. The light, coming from the opposite direction, fell on her face.

'My wife started up, and, grasping my hand, asked: "O ke?" [Footnote: 'O ke?' is the Bengali for 'Who is that?'] In her feeble condition, she was so startled to see a stranger standing at the door that she asked two or three times in a hoarse whisper: "O ke? O ke? O ke?"

'At first I answered weakly: "I do not know"; but the next moment I felt as though some one had whipped me, and I hastily corrected myself and said: "Why, it's our doctor's daughter."

'My wife turned and looked at me. I was not able to look her in the face. Then she turned to the new-comer, and said in a weak voice: "Come in," and turning to me added: "Bring the lamp."

'Monorama came into the room, and began to talk a little to my wife. While she was talking the doctor came to see his patient.

'He had brought with him from the dispensary two bottles of medicine. Taking these out he said to my wife: "See, this blue bottle is for outward application, and the other is to be taken. Be careful not to mix the two, for this is a deadly poison."

'Warning me also, he placed the two bottles on the table by the bedside. When he was going the doctor called his daughter.

'She said to him: "Father, why should I not stay? There is no woman here to nurse her."

'My wife got quite excited and sat up saying: "No, no, don't you bother yourself. I have an old maidservant who takes care of me as if she were my mother."

'Just as the doctor was going away with his daughter, my wife said to him: "Doctor, he has been sitting too long in this close and stuffy room. Won't you take him out for some fresh air?"

'The doctor turned to me, and said: "Come along, I'll take you for a stroll along the bank of the river."

'After some little show of unwillingness I agreed. Before going the doctor again warned my wife about the two bottles of medicine.

'That evening I took my dinner at the doctor's house, and was late in coming home. On getting back I found that my wife was in extreme pain. Feeling deeply repentant, I asked her: "Has your pain increased?"

'She was too ill to answer, but only looked up in my face. I saw that she was breathing with difficulty.

'I at once sent for the doctor.

'At first he could not make out what was the matter. At last he asked: "Has that pain increased? Haven't you used that liniment?"

'Saying which, he picked up the blue bottle from the table. It was empty!

'Showing signs of agitation, he asked my wife: "You haven't taken this medicine by mistake, have you?" Nodding her head, she silently indicated that she had.

'The doctor ran out of the house to bring his stomach pump, and I fell on the bed like one insensible.

'Then, just as a mother tries to pacify a sick child, my wife drew my head to her breast, and with the touch of her hands attempted to tell me her thoughts. Merely by that tender touch, she said to me again and again: "Do not sorrow, all is for the best. You will be happy, and knowing that I die happily."

'By the time the doctor returned, all my wife's pains had ceased with her life.'

Dokhin Babu, taking another gulp of water, exclaimed: 'Ugh, it's terribly hot,' and then, going on to the veranda, he paced rapidly up and down two or three times. Coming back he sat down, and began again. It was clear enough that he did not want to tell me; but it seemed as if, by some sort of magic, I was dragging the story out of him. He went on:

'After my marriage with Monorama, whenever I tried to talk effusively to her, she looked grave. It seemed as if there was in her mind some hint of suspicion which I could not understand.

'It was at this time that I began to have a fondness for drink.

'One evening in the early autumn, I was strolling with Monorama in our garden by the river. The darkness had the feeling of a phantom world about it, and there was not even the occasional sound of the birds rustling their wings in their sleep. Only on both sides of the path along which we were walking the tops of the casuarina trees sighed in the breeze.

'Feeling tired, Monorama went and lay down on that marble slab, placing her hands behind her head, and I sat beside her.

'There the darkness seemed to be even denser, and the only patch of sky that could be seen was thick with stars. The chirping of the crickets under the trees was like a thin hem of sound at the lowest edge of the skirt of silence.

'That evening I had been drinking a little, and my heart was in a melting mood. When my eyes had got used to the darkness, the grey outline of the loosely clad and languid form of Monorama, lying in the shadow of the trees, awakened in my mind an undefinable longing. It seemed to me as if she were only an unsubstantial shadow which I could never grasp in my arms.

'Suddenly the tops of the casuarina trees seemed to be on fire. I saw the jagged edge of the old moon, golden in her harvest hue, rise gradually above the tops of the trees. The moonlight fell on the face of the white-clad form lying on the white marble. I could contain myself no longer. Drawing near her and taking her hand in mine, I said: "Monorama, you may not believe me, but never shall I be able to forget your love."

'The moment the words were out of my mouth I started, for I remembered that I had used the very same to someone else long before. And at the same time, from over the top of the casuarina trees, from under the golden crescent of the old moon, from across the wide stretches of the flowing Ganges, right to its most distant bank - Ha ha Ha ha Ha ha - came the sound of laughter passing swiftly overhead. Whether it was a heart-breaking laugh or a sky-rending wail, I cannot say. But on hearing it I fell to the ground in a swoon.

'When I recovered consciousness, I saw that I was lying on my bed in my own room. My wife asked me: "Whatever happened to you?" I replied, trembling with terror: "Didn't you hear how the whole sky rang with the sound of laughter - Ha ha Ha ha Ha ha? "My wife laughed, as she answered: "Laughter? What I heard was the sound of a flock of birds flying past overhead. You are easily frightened!"

'Next day I knew quite well that it was a flock of ducks migrating, as they do at that time of year, to the south. But when evening came I began to doubt again, and in my imagination the whole sky rang with laughter, piercing the darkness on the least pretext. It came to this at last that after dark I was not able to speak a word to Monorama.

'Then I decided to leave my garden-house, and took Monorama for a trip on the river. In the keen November air all my fear left me, and for some days I was quite happy.

'Leaving the Ganges, and crossing the river Khore, we at last reached the Padma. This terrible river lay stretched out like a huge serpent taking its winter sleep. On its north side were the barren, solitary sand-banks, which lay blazing in the sun; and on the high banks of the south side the mango groves of the villages stood close to the open jaws of this demoniac river, which now and again turned in its sleep, whereupon the cracked earth of the banks fell with a thud into its waters.

'Finding a suitable place, I moored the boat to the bank.

'One day we went out for a walk, on and on, till we were far away from our boat. The golden light of the setting sun gradually faded, and the sky was flooded with the pure silver light of the moon. As the moonlight fell on that limitless expanse of white sand, and filled the vast sky with its flood of brilliance, I felt as if we two were all alone, wandering in an uninhabited, unbounded dreamland, and without purpose. Monorama was wearing a red shawl, which she pulled over her head, and wrapped round her shoulders, leaving only her face visible. When the silence became deeper, and there was nothing but a vastness of white solitude all around us, then Mono-rama slowly put out her hand and took hold of mine. She seemed so close to me that I felt as if she had surrendered into my hands her body and mind, her life and youth. In my yearning and happy heart, I said to myself: "Is there room enough anywhere else than under such a wide, open sky to contain the hearts of two human beings in love?" Then I felt as if we had no home to return to, that we could go on wandering thus, hand in hand, free from all cares and obstacles, along a road which had no end, through the moonlit immensity.

'As we went on, we came at last to a place where I could see a pool of water surrounded by hillocks of sand.

'Through the heart of this still water a long beam of moonlight pierced, like a flashing sword. Arriving at the edge of the pool, we stood there in silence, and Monorama looked up into my face. Her shawl slipped from off her head, and I stooped down and kissed her.

'Just then there came, from somewhere in the midst of that silent and solitary desert, a voice, saying three times in solemn tones: "O ke? O ke? O ke?"

'I started back, and my wife also trembled. But the next moment both of us realised that the sound was neither human nor superhuman it was the call of some water-fowl, startled from its sleep at the sound of strangers so late at night near its nest.

'Recovering from our fright, we returned as fast as we could to the boat. Being late, we went straight to bed, and Monorama was soon fast asleep.

'Then in the darkness it seemed as if someone, standing by the side of the bed, was pointing a long, thin finger towards the sleeping Monorama, and with a hoarse whisper was asking me over and over again: "O ke? O ke? O ke?"

'Hastily getting up, I seized a box of matches, and lighted the lamp. Just as I did so, the mosquito net began to flutter in the wind, and the boat began to rock. The blood in my veins curdled, and the sweat came in heavy drops as I heard an echoing laugh, "Ha ha, Ha ha, Ha ha," sound through the dark night. It travelled over the river, across the sand-banks on the other side, and after that it passed over all the sleeping country, the villages and the towns, as though forever crossing the countries of this and other worlds. Fainter and fainter it grew, passing into limitless space, gradually becoming fine as the point of a needle. Never had I heard such a piercingly faint sound, never had I imagined such a ghost of a sound possible. It was as if within my skull there was the limitless sky of space, and no matter how far the sound travelled it could not get outside my brain.

'At last, when it was almost unbearable, I thought, unless I extinguished the light, I should not be able to sleep. No sooner had I put out the lamp than once more, close to my mosquito curtain, I heard in the darkness that hoarse voice saying: "O ke? O ke? O ke?" My heart began to beat in unison with the words, and gradually began to repeat the question: "O ke? O ke? O ke?" In the silence of the night, from the middle of the boat my round clock began to be eloquent, and, pointing its hour hand towards Monorama, ticked out the question: "O ke? O ke? O ke?"' As he spoke, Dokhin Babu became ghastly pale, and his voice seemed to be choking him. Touching him on the shoulder, I said: 'Take a little water.' At the same moment the kerosene lamp flickered and went out, and I saw that outside it was light. A crow cawed, and a yellow-hammer whistled. On the road in front of my house the creaking of a bullock-cart was heard.

The expression on Dokhin Babu's face was altogether changed. There was no longer the least trace of fear. That he had told me so much under the intoxication of an imaginary fear, and deluded by the sorcery of night, seemed to make him very much ashamed, and even angry with me. Without any formality of farewell he jumped up, and shot out of the house.

Next night, when it was quite late, I was again wakened from my sleep by a voice calling: 'Doctor, Doctor.'

THE FUGITIVE GOLD

I

After his father's death, Baidyanath settled down on the proceeds of the Government stock which had been left to him. It never even occurred to him to look for work. His manner of spending time was to cut off branches of trees, and with minute care and skill he would polish them into walking-sticks. The boys and young men of the neighbourhood were candidates for these, and his supply of them never fell short of the demand.

By the blessing of the God of Fruition, Baidyanath had two boys and one daughter who had been given in marriage at the proper time.

But his wife Sundari bore a grievance against her lot, because there was not the same surplus in the resources of her husband as in those of their cousin across the road. The dispensation of Providence struck her as unnecessarily imperfect, when she could not show the same glitter of gold in her house, and tilt her nose as superciliously as her neighbour.

The condition of her own house gave her continual annoyance, where things were not only inconvenient but humiliating. Her bedstead, she was sure, was not decent enough to carry a corpse, and even an orphan bat who for seven generations had been without relatives would have scorned to accept an invitation within such dilapidated walls; while as for the furniture, why, it would have brought tears to the eyes of the most hardened of ascetics. It is impossible for a cowardly sex like man to argue against such palpable exaggerations, so Baidyanath merely retired on to his veranda, and worked with redoubled energy at polishing his walking-sticks.

But the rampart of silence is not the surest means of self-defence. Sometimes the wife would break upon her husband at his work, and, without looking at him, say: 'Please tell the milkman to stop delivering milk.'

At which Baidyanath, after his first shock of speechlessness, might possibly stammer out: 'Milk? How can you get on if you stop the supply? What will the children drink?'

To this his wife would answer: 'Rice water.' On another day she would use quite the opposite method of attack, and, suddenly bursting into the room, would exclaim: 'I give it up, you manage your own household.'

Baidyanath would mutter in despair: 'What do you wish me to do?'

His wife would reply: 'You do the marketing for this month,' and then give him a list of materials sufficient for reckless orgies of feasting.

If Baidyanath could summon up courage to ask: 'What is the necessity of so much?' he would get the reply:

'Indeed it will be cheaper for you to let the children die of starvation, and me also for that matter.'

II

One day after finishing his morning meal Baidyanath was sitting alone, preparing the thread for a kite, when he saw one of those wandering mendicants, who are reputed to know the secret of transmuting the baser metals into gold. In a moment there flashed to his mind the surest chance of unearned increment to his funds. He took the mendicant into his house, and was surprised at his own cleverness when he secured the consent of his guest to teach him the art of making gold. After having swallowed an alarming amount of nourishment, and a considerable portion of Baidyanath's paternal inheritance, the ascetic at last encouraged Baidyanath and his wife with the hope that the next day they would see their dream realised.

That night no one had any sleep. The husband and wife, with astounding prodigality, began to build golden castles in the air and discuss the details of the architecture. Their conjugal harmony was so unusually perfect for that night that in spite of disagreements they were willing to allow compromises in their plans for each other's sake.

Next day the magician had mysteriously disappeared, and with him the golden haze from the atmosphere in which they had been living. The sunlight itself appeared dark, and the house and its furniture seemed to its mistress to be four times more disgraceful than before.

Henceforth, if Baidyanath ventured even a truism on the most trifling or household matters, his wife would advise him with withering sarcasm to be careful of the last remnant of his intelligence after the reckless expenditure from which it had suffered.

Sundari in the meantime was showing her hand to every palmist that came her way, and also her horoscope. She was told that in the matter of children she would be fortunate, and that her house would soon be filled with sons and daughters. But such prospect of overgrowth of population in her house did not produce any exhilaration in her mind.

At last one day an astrologer came and said that if within a year her husband did not come upon some hidden treasure, then he would throw his science to the winds and go about begging. Hearing him speak with such desperate certainty, Sundari could not entertain a moment's doubt as to the truth of his prophecy.

There are certain recognised methods for acquiring wealth, such as agriculture, service, trade, and the legal and illegal professions. But none of these points out the direction of hidden wealth. Therefore, while his wife spurred him on, it more and more perplexed him to decide upon the particular mound which he should excavate, or the part of the river-bed where he should send down a diver to search.

In the meantime the Poojah Festival was approaching. A week before the day, boats began to arrive at the village landing laden with passengers returning home with their purchases: baskets full of vegetables, tin trunks filled with new shoes, umbrellas and clothes for the children, scents and soap, the latest story-books, and perfumed oil for the wives.

The light of the autumn sun filled the cloudless sky with the gladness of festival, and the ripe paddy fields shimmered in the sun, while the cocoa-nut leaves washed by the rains rustled in the fresh cool breeze.

The children, getting up very early, went to see the image of the goddess which was being prepared in the courtyard of the neighbouring house. When it was their meal-time, the maid-servant had to come and drag them away by force. At that time Baidyanath was brooding over the futility of his own life, amidst this universal stir of merriment in the neighbourhood. Taking his two children from the servant, he drew them towards him, and asked the elder one: 'Well, Obu, tell me what do you want for a present this time?'

Obu replied without a moment's hesitation: 'Give me a toy boat, father.'

The younger one, not wishing to be behindhand with his brother, said: 'Oh, father, do give me a toy boat too.'

III

At this time an uncle of Sundari's had come to his house from Benares, where he was working as an advocate, and Sundari spent a great part of her time going round to see him.

At last one day she said to her husband: 'Look here, you will have to go to Benares.'

Baidyanath at once concluded that his wife had received from an astrologer a positive assurance of his impending death, and was anxious for him to die in that holy place, to secure better advantage in the next world.

Then he was told that at Benares there was a house in which rumour said there was some hidden treasure. Surely it was destined for him to buy that house and secure the treasure.

Baidyanath, in a fit of desperation, tried to assert his independence, and exclaimed: 'Good heavens, I cannot go to Benares.'

Two days passed, during which Baidyanath was busily engaged in making toy boats. He fixed masts in them, and fastened sails, hoisted a red flag, and put in rudders and oars. He did not even forget steersmen and passengers to boot. It would have been difficult to find a boy, even in these modern times, cynical enough to despise such a gift. And when Baidyanath, the night before the festival, gave these boats to his boys, they became wild with delight.

On hearing their shouts Sundari came in, and at the sight of these gifts flew into a fury of rage, and, seizing the toys, threw them out of the window.

The younger child began to scream with disappointment, and his mother, giving him a resounding box on the ears, said: 'Stop your silly noise.'

The elder boy, when he saw his father's face, forgot his own disappointment, and with an appearance of cheerfulness said: 'Never mind, father, I will go and fetch them first thing in the morning.'

Next day Baidyanath agreed to go to Benares. He took the children in his arms, and kissing them good-bye, left the house.

IV

The house at Benares belonged to a client of his wife's uncle, and for that reason perhaps the price was fairly high. Baidyanath took possession of it, and began to live there alone. It was situated right on the river-bank, and its walls were washed by the current.

At night Baidyanath began to have an eerie feeling, and he drew his sheet over his head, but could not sleep. When in the depth of night all was still he was suddenly startled to hear a clanking sound from somewhere. It was faint but clear, as though in the nether regions the treasurer of the god Mammon was counting out his money.

Baidyanath was terrified, but with the fear there mingled curiosity and the hope of success. With trembling hand he carried the lamp from room to room, to discover the place where the sound had its origin, till in the morning it became inaudible among the other noises.

The next day at midnight the sound was heard again, and Baidyanath felt like a traveller in a desert, who can hear the gurgle of water without knowing from which direction it is coming, hesitating to move a step, for the fear of taking a wrong path and going farther away from the spring.

Many days passed in this anxious manner, until his face, usually so serenely content, became lined with anxiety and care. His eyes were sunk in their sockets, and had a hungry look, with a glow like that of the burning sand of the desert under the mid-day sun.

At last one night a happy thought came to him, and locking all the doors, he began to strike the floors of all the rooms with a crowbar. >From the floor of one small room came a hollow sound. He began to dig. It was nearly dawn when the digging was completed.

Through the opening made Baidyanath saw that underneath there was a chamber, but in the darkness he had not the courage to take a jump into the unknown. He placed his bedstead over the entrance, and lay down. So morning came. That day, even in the day-time, the sound could be heard. Repeating the name of Durga, he dragged his bedstead away from the cavity in the floor. The splash of lapping water and the clank of metal became louder. Fearfully peeping through the hole into the darkness, he could see that the chamber was full of flowing water, which, when examined with a stick, was found to be about a couple of feet deep. Taking a box of matches and a lantern in his hand, he easily jumped into the shallow room. But lest in one moment all his hopes should collapse, his trembling hand found it difficult to light the lantern. After striking almost a whole box of matches, he at last succeeded.

He saw by its light a large copper cauldron, fastened to a thick iron chain. Every now and then, when the current came with a rush, the chain clanked against the side, and made the metallic sound which he had heard.

Baidyanath waded quickly through the water, and went up to this vessel, only to find that it was empty.

He could not believe his eyes, and with both hands he took the cauldron up and shook it furiously. He turned it upside down, but in vain. He saw that its mouth was broken, as though at one time this vessel had been closed and sealed, and someone had broken it open.

Baidyanath began to grope about in the water. Something struck against his hand, which on lifting he found to be a skull. He held it up to his ear, and shook it violently, but it was empty. He threw it down.

He saw that on one side of the room towards the river the wall was broken. It was through this opening that the water entered, and he felt sure that it had been made by his unknown predecessor, who had a more reliable horoscope than his own.

At last, having lost all hope, he heaved a deep sigh, which seemed to mingle with the innumerable sighs of despair coming from some subterranean inferno of everlasting failures.

His whole body besmeared with mud, Baid-yanath made his way up into the house. The world, full of its bustling population, seemed to him empty as that broken vessel and chained to a meaningless destiny.

Once more to pack his things, to buy his ticket, to get into the train, to return again to his home, to have to wrangle with his wife, and to endure the burden of his sordid days, all this seemed to him intolerably unreasonable. He wished that he could just slide into the water, as the broken-down bank of a river into the passing current.

Still he did pack his things, buy his ticket, get into the train, and one evening at the end of a winter day arrive at his home.

On entering the house, he sat like one dazed in the courtyard, not venturing to go into the inner apartments. The old maid-servant was the first to catch sight of him, and at her shout of surprise the children came running to see him with their glad laughter. Then his wife called him.

Baidyanath started up as if from sleep, and once more woke into the life which he had lived before. With sad face and wan smile, he took one of the boys in his arms and the other by the hand and entered the room. The lamps had just been lighted, and although it was not yet night, it was a cold evening, and everything was as quiet as if night had come.

Baidyanath remained silent for a little, and then in a soft voice said to his wife: 'How are you?'

His wife, without making any reply, asked him: 'What has happened?'

Baidyanath, without speaking, simply struck his forehead. At this Sundari's face hardened. The children, feeling the shadow of a calamity, quietly slipped away, and going to the maidservant asked her to tell them a story.

Night fell, but neither husband nor wife spoke a word. The whole atmosphere of the house seemed to palpitate with silence, and gradually Sundari's lips set hard like a miser's purse. Then she got up, and leaving her husband went slowly into her bedroom, locking the door behind her. Baidyanath remained standing silently outside. The watchman's call was heard as he passed. The tired world was sunk in deep sleep.

When it was quite late at night the elder boy, wakened from some dream, left his bed, and coming out on to the veranda whispered: 'Father.'

But his father was not there. In a slightly raised voice he called from outside the closed door of his parents' bedroom, 'Father,' but he got no answer. And in fear he went back to bed.

Next morning early the maid-servant, according to her custom, prepared her master's tobacco, and went in search of him, but could find him nowhere.

THE EDITOR

As long as my wife was alive, I did not pay much attention to Probha. As a matter of fact, I thought a great deal more about Probha's mother than I did of the child herself.

At that time my dealing with her was superficial, limited to a little petting, listening to her lisping chatter, and occasionally watching her laugh and play. As long as it was agreeable to me I used to fondle her, but as soon as it threatened to become tiresome I would surrender her to her mother with the greatest readiness.

At last, on the untimely death of my wife, the child dropped from her mother's arms into mine, and I took her to my heart.

But it is difficult to say whether it was I who considered it my duty to bring up the motherless child with twofold care, or my daughter who thought it her duty to take care of her wifeless father with a superfluity of attention. At any rate, it is a fact that from the age of six she began to assume the rele of housekeeper. It was quite clear that this little girl constituted herself the sole guardian of her father.

I smiled inwardly but surrendered myself completely to her hands. I soon saw that the more inefficient and helpless I was the better pleased she became. I found that even if I took down my own clothes from the peg, or went to get my own umbrella, she put on such an air of offended dignity that it was clear that she thought I had usurped her right. Never before had she possessed such a perfect doll as she now had in her father, and so she took the keenest pleasure in feeding him, dressing him, and even putting him to bed. Only when I was teaching her the elements of arithmetic or the First Reader had I the opportunity of summoning up my parental authority.

Every now and then the thought troubled me as to where I should be able to get enough money to provide her with a dowry for a suitable bridegroom. I was giving her a good education, but what would happen if she fell into the hands of an ignorant fool?

I made up my mind to earn money. I was too old to get employment in a Government office, and I had not the influence to get work in a private one. After a good deal of thought I decided that I would write books.

If you make holes in a bamboo tube, it will no longer hold either oil or water, in fact its power of receptivity is lost; but if you blow through it, then, without any expenditure it may produce music. I felt quite sure that the man who is not useful can be ornamental, and he who is not productive in other fields can at least produce literature. Encouraged by this thought, I wrote a farce. People said it was good, and it was even acted on the stage.

Once having tasted of fame, I found myself unable to stop pursuing it farther. Days and days together I went on writing farces with an agony of determination.

Probha would come with her smile, and remind me gently: 'Father, it is time for you to take your bath.'

And I would growl out at her: 'Go away, go away; can't you see that I am busy now? Don't vex me.'

The poor child would leave me, unnoticed, with a face dark like a lamp whose light has been suddenly blown out.

I drove the maid-servants away, and beat the men-servants, and when beggars came and sang at my door I would get up and run after them with a stick. My room being by the side of the street, passers-by would stop and ask me to tell them the way, but I would request them to go to Jericho. Alas, no one took it into serious consideration that I was engaged in writing a screaming farce.

Yet I never got money in the measure that I got fun and fame. But that did not trouble me, although in the meantime all the potential bridegrooms were growing up for other brides whose parents did not write farces.

But just then an excellent opportunity came my way. The landlord of a certain village, Jahirgram, started a newspaper, and sent a request that I would become its editor. I agreed to take the post.

For the first few days I wrote with such fire and zest that people used to point at me when I went out into the street, and I began to feel a brilliant halo about my forehead.

Next to Jahirgram was the village of Ahirgram. Between the landlords of these two villages there was a constant rivalry and feud. There had been a time when they came to blows not infrequently. But now, since the magistrate had bound them both over to keep the peace, I took the place of the hired ruffians who used to act for one of the rivals. Every one said that I lived up to the dignity of my position.

My writings were so strong and fiery that Ahirgram could no longer hold up its head. I blackened with my ink the whole of their ancient clan and family.

All this time I had the comfortable feeling of being pleased with myself. I even became fat. My face beamed with the exhilaration of a successful man of genius. I admired my own delightful ingenuity of insinuation, when at some excruciating satire of mine, directed against the ancestry of Ahirgram, the whole of Jahirgram would burst its sides with laughter like an over-ripe melon. I enjoyed myself thoroughly.

But at last Ahirgram started a newspaper. What it published was starkly naked, without a shred of literary urbanity. The language it used was of such undiluted colloquialism that every letter seemed to scream in one's face. The consequence was that the inhabitants of both villages clearly understood its meaning.

But as I was hampered in my style by my sense of decency, my subtlety of sarcasm very often made but a feeble impression upon the power of understanding of both my friends and my enemies.

The result was that even when I won decidedly in this war of infamy my readers were not aware of my victory. At last in desperation I wrote a sermon on the necessity of good taste in literature, but found that I had made a fatal mistake. For things that are solemn offer more surface for ridicule than things that are truly ridiculous. And therefore my effort at the moral betterment of my fellow-beings had the opposite effect to that which I had intended.

My employer ceased to show me such attention as he had done. The honour to which I had grown accustomed dwindled in its quantity, and its quality became poor. When I walked in the street people did not go out of their way to carry off the memory of a word with me. They even went so far as to be frivolously familiar in their behaviour towards me, such as slapping my shoulders with a laugh and giving me nicknames.

In the meantime my admirers had quite forgotten the farces which had made me famous. I felt as if I was a burnt-out match, charred to its very end.

My mind became so depressed that, no matter how I racked my brains, I was unable to write one line. I seemed to have lost all zest for life.

Probha had now grown afraid of me. She would not venture to approach me unless summoned. She had come to understand that a commonplace doll is a far better companion than a genius of a father who writes comic pieces.

One day I saw that the Ahirgram newspaper, leaving my employer alone for once, had directed its attack on me. Some very ugly imputations had been made against myself. One by one all my friends and acquaintances came and read to me the spiciest bits, laughing heartily. Some of them said that however one might disagree with the subject-matter, it could not be denied that it was cleverly written. In the course of the day at least twenty people came and said the same thing, with slight variations to break its monotony.

In front of my house there is a small garden. I was walking there in the evening with a mind distracted with pain. When the birds had returned to their nests, and surrendered themselves to the peace of the evening, I understood quite clearly that amongst the birds at any rate there were no writers of journalism, nor did they hold discussions on good taste. I was thinking only of one thing, namely, what answer I could make. The disadvantage of politeness is that it is not intelligible to all classes of people. So I had decided that my answer must be given in the same strain as the attack. I was not going to allow myself to acknowledge defeat.

Just as I had come to this conclusion, a well-known voice came softly through the darkness of the evening, and immediately afterwards I felt a soft warm touch in the palm of my hand. I was so distracted and absent-minded that even though that voice and touch were familiar to me, I did not realise that I knew them.

But the next moment, when they had left me, the voice sounded in my ear, and the memory of the touch became living. My child had slowly come near to me once more, and had whispered in my ear, 'Father,' but not getting any answer she had lifted my right hand, and with it had gently stroked her forehead, and then silently gone back into the house.

For a long time Probha had not called me like that, nor caressed me with such freedom. Therefore it was that to-day at the touch of her love my heart suddenly began to yearn for her. Going back to the house a little later, I saw that Probha was lying on her bed. Her eyes were half closed, and she seemed to be in pain. She lay like a flower which has dropped on the dust at the end of the day.

Putting my hand on her forehead, I found that she was feverish. Her breath was hot, and her pulse was throbbing.

I realised that the poor child, feeling the first symptoms of fever, had come with her thirsty heart to get her father's love and caresses, while he was trying to think of some stinging reply to send to the newspaper.

I sat beside her. The child, without speaking a word, took my hand between her two fever-heated palms, and laid it upon her forehead, lying quite still.

All the numbers of the Jahirgram and Ahirgram papers which I had in the house I burnt to ashes. I wrote no answer to the attack. Never had I felt such joy as I did, when I thus acknowledged defeat.

I had taken the child to my arms when her mother had died, and now, having cremated this rival of her mother, again I took her to my heart.

GIRIBALA

I

Giribala is overflowing with the exuberance of her youth that seems spilling over all around her, in the folds of her dress, the turning of her neck, the motion of her hands, in the rhythm of her steps, now quick, now languid, in her tinkling anklets and ringing laughter, in her voice and her swift glances. Often she is seen, wrapt in a blue silk, walking on her terrace, in an impulse of unmeaning restlessness. Her limbs seem eager to dance to the time of an inner music unceasing and unheard. She takes pleasure in merely moving her body, causing ripples to break out in the flood of her young life. Suddenly she will pluck a leaf from a plant in the flower-pot, and throw it up in the sky, and her bangles give a sudden tinkle and the careless grace of her hand, like a bird freed from its cage, flies unseen in the air. With her swift fingers she brushes away from her dress a mere nothing; standing on tiptoe she peeps over her terrace walls for no cause whatever, and then with a rapid motion turns round to go to another direction, swinging her bunch of keys tied to a corner of her garment. She loosens her hair in an untimely caprice, sitting before her mirror to do it up again, and then in a fit of laziness flings herself upon her bed like a line of stray moonlight, slipping through some opening of the leaves, idling in the shadow.

She has no children and, having been married into a wealthy family, has very little work to do. Thus she seems daily accumulating her own self without expenditure till the vessel is brimming over with the seething surplus. She has her husband, but not under her control. She has grown up from a girl into a woman, and yet through familiarity escaping her husband's notice.

When she was newly married, and her husband, Gopinath, was attending his college, he would often play the truant and, under cover of the mid-day siesta of his elders, secretly come to make love to Giribala. Though they lived under the same roof he would create occasions to send her letters on tinted notepaper perfumed with rosewater, and even would gloat upon exaggerated grievances over some imaginary neglect of love.

Just then his father died, and he became the sole owner of his property. Like an unseasoned piece of timber, the immature youth of Gopinath attracted parasites that began to bore into his substance. >From now his movements took the course which led him in a contrary direction from his wife.

There is a dangerous fascination in being a leader of men, to which has succumbed many a strong soul. To be accepted as the leader of a small circle of sycophants in his own parlour has the same fearful attraction for a man who suffers from a scarcity of brains and character. Gopinath assumed the part of a hero among his friends and acquaintances, and tried daily to invent new wonders in all manner of extravagance. He won a reputation among his followers for his audacity of excesses, which goaded him not only to keep up his fame but to surpass himself at all costs.

In the meanwhile, Giribala in the seclusion of her lonely youth felt like a queen who had her throne but no subjects. She knew she had the power in her hand which could make the world of men her captive, only that world itself was missing. Giribala has a maid-servant whose name is Sudha. She can sing and dance and improvise verses, and she freely gives expression to her regret that such a beauty as that of her mistress should be dedicated to a fool who forgets to enjoy that which he has in his possession. Giribala is never tired of hearing from her the details of her charms of beauty, while at the same time contradicting her, calling her a liar and flatterer, exciting her to swear by all that is sacred that she is earnest in her admiration, which statement, even without the accompaniment of a solemn oath, is not difficult for Giribala to believe.

Sudha used to sing to her a song beginning with the line, 'Let me write myself a slave upon the soles of thy feet,' and Giribala in her imagination could feel that her beautiful feet were fully worthy of bearing inscriptions of everlasting slavery from conquered hearts, if only they could be free in their career of conquest.

But the woman to whom her husband Gopinath has surrendered himself as a slave is Lavanga, the actress, who has the reputation of playing to perfection the part of a maiden languishing in hopeless love, and swooning on the stage with an exquisite naturalness. Before her husband had altogether vanished from her sphere of influence, Giribala had often heard from him about the wonderful histrionic powers of this woman, and in her jealous curiosity had greatly desired to see Lavanga on the stage. But she could not secure her husband's consent, because Gopinath was firm in his opinion that the theatre was a place not fit for any decent woman to visit.

At last she paid for a seat, and sent Sudha to see this famous actress in one of her best parts. The account that she received from her on her return was far from flattering to Lavanga, either as to her personal appearance or as to her stage accomplishments. Since, for obvious reasons, she had great faith in Sudha's power of appreciation where it was due, she did not hesitate to believe in her description of Lavanga which was accompanied by mimicry of a ludicrous mannerism.

When at last her husband deserted her in his infatuation for this woman, she began to feel qualms of doubt. But as Sudha repeatedly asserted her former opinion with a greater vehemence, comparing Lavanga to a piece of burnt log dressed up in a woman's clothes, Giribala determined secretly to go to the theatre herself and settle this question for good. And she did go there one night with all the excitement of a forbidden entry. Her very trepidation of heart lent a special charm to what she saw there. She gazed at the faces of the spectators, lit up with an unnatural shine of lamplight; and, with the magic of its music and the painted canvas of its scenery, the theatre seemed to her like a world where society was suddenly freed from its law of gravitation.

Coming from her walled-up terrace and joyless home, she had entered a region where dreams and reality had clasped their hands in friendship, over the wine-cup of art.

The bell rang, the orchestra music stopped, the audience sat still in their seats, the stage lights shone brighter, and the curtain was drawn up. Suddenly appeared in the light from the mystery of the unseen the shepherd girls of the Vrinda forest, and with the accompaniment of songs commenced their dance, punctuated with the uproarious applause of the audience. The blood began to throb all over Giribala's body, and she forgot for the moment that her life was limited to her circumstances, and that she had not been set free in a world where all laws had melted in music.

Sudha came occasionally to interrupt her with anxious whispers, urging her to hasten back home for fear of being detected. But she paid no heed to the warning, for her sense of fear had gone.

The play goes on. Krishna has given offence to his beloved Radha, and she in her wounded pride refuses to recognise him. He is entreating her, abasing himself at her feet, but in vain. Giribala's heart seems to swell. She imagines herself as the offended Radha; and feels that she also has in her this woman's power to vindicate her pride. She had heard what a force was woman's beauty in the world, but to-night it became to her palpable.

At last the curtain dropped, the light became dim, the audience got ready to leave the theatre, but Giribala sat still like one in a dream. The thought that she would have to go home had vanished from her mind. She waited for the curtain to rise again and the eternal theme of Krishna's humiliation at the feet of Radha to continue. But Sudha came to remind her that the play had ended, and the lamps would soon be put out.

It was late when Giribala came back home. A kerosene lamp was dimly burning in the melancholy solitude and silence of her room. Near her window upon her lonely bed a mosquito curtain was slightly moving in a gentle breeze. Her world seemed to her distasteful and mean, like a rotten fruit swept into the dustbin.

>From now she regularly visited the theatre every Saturday. The fascination of her first sight of it lost much of its glamour. The painted vulgarity of the actresses and the falseness of their affectation became more and more evident, yet the habit grew upon her. Every time the curtain rose the window of her life's prison-house seemed to open before her, and the stage, bordered off from the world of reality by its gilded frame and scenic display, by its array of lights and even its flimsiness of conventionalism, appeared to her like a fairyland, where it was not impossible for herself to occupy the throne of the fairy queen.

When for the first time she saw her husband among the audience shouting his drunken admiration for a certain actress, she felt an intense disgust, and prayed in her mind that a day might come when she might have an opportunity to spurn him away with her contempt. But the opportunity seemed remoter every day, for Gopinath was hardly ever to be seen at his home now, being carried away, one knew not where, in the centre of a dust-storm of dissipation.

One evening in the month of March, in the light of the full moon, Giribala was sitting on her terrace dressed in her cream-coloured robe. It was her habit daily to deck herself with jewelry, as if for some festive occasion. For these costly gems were like wine to her, they sent heightened consciousness of beauty to her limbs; she felt like a plant in spring tingling with the impulse of flowers in all its branches. She wore a pair of diamond bracelets on her arms, a necklace of rubies and pearls on her neck, and a ring with a big sapphire on the little finger of her left hand. Sudha was sitting near her bare feet, admiringly touching them with her hand, and expressing her wish that she were a man privileged to offer his life as homage to such a pair of feet.

Sudha gently hummed a love-song to her, and the evening wore on to night. Everybody in the household had finished the evening meal, and gone to sleep. Then suddenly Gopinath appeared reeking with scent and liquor, and Sudha, drawing her sari over her face, hastily ran away from the terrace.

Giribala thought for a moment that her day had come at last. She turned away her face, and sat silent.

But the curtain in her stage did not rise, and no song of entreaty came from her hero with the words:

Listen to the pleading of the moonlight, my love, and hide not thy face.

In his dry unmusical voice Gopinath said: 'Give me your keys.'

A gust of south wind like a sigh of the insulted romance of the poetic world scattered all over the terrace the smell of the night-blooming jasmines, and loosened some wisp of hair on Giribala's cheek. She let go her pride, and got up and said: 'You shall have your keys if you listen to >what I have to say.'

Gopinath said: 'I cannot delay. Give me your keys.'

Giribala said: 'I will give you the keys and everything that is in the safe, but you must not leave me.'

Gopinath said: 'That cannot be. I have urgent business.'

'Then you shan't have the keys,' said Giribala.

Gopinath began to search for them. He opened the drawers of the dressing-table, broke open the lid of the box that contained Giribala's toilet requisites, smashed the glass panes of her almirah, groped under the pillows and mattress of the bed, but the keys he could not find. Giribala stood near the door stiff and silent, like a marble image gazing at vacancy. Trembling with rage, Gopinath came to her, and said with an angry growl: 'Give me your keys or you will repent it.'

Giribala did not answer, and Gopinath, pinning her to the wall, snatched away by force her bracelets, necklace and ring, and, giving her a parting kick, went away.

Nobody in the house woke up from his sleep, none in the neighbourhood knew of this outrage, the moonlight remained placid, and the peace of the night undisturbed. Hearts can be rent never to heal again amidst such serene silence.

The next morning Giribala said she was going to see her father, and left home. As Gopinath's present destination was not known, and she was not responsible to anybody else in the house, her absence was not noticed.

II

The new play of Manorama was on rehearsal in the theatre where Gopinath was a constant visitor. Lavanga was practising for the part of the heroine Manorama, and Gopinath, sitting in the front seat with his rabble of followers, would vociferously encourage his favourite actress with his approbation. This greatly disturbed the rehearsal, but the proprietors of the theatre did not dare to annoy a patron of whose vindictiveness they were afraid. But one day he went so far as to molest an actress in the green-room, and he had to be turned away with the aid of the police.

Gopinath determined to take his revenge, and when, after a great deal of preparation and shrieking advertisements, the new play Manorama was about to be produced, Gopinath took away the principal actress Lavanga with him, and disappeared. It was a great shock to the manager, who had to postpone the opening night, get hold of a new actress, and teach her the part, bringing out the play before the public with considerable misgivings in his mind.

But the success was as unexpected as it was unprecedented. When the news reached Gopinath, he could not resist the curiosity to come and see the performance.

The play opens with Manorama living in her husband's house neglected and hardly noticed. Near the end of the drama her husband deserts her, and, concealing his first marriage, manages to marry a millionaire's daughter. When the wedding ceremony is over, and the bridal veil is raised from her face, she is discovered to be the same Manorama, only no longer the former drudge, but queenly in her beauty and splendour of dress and ornaments. In her infancy she had been brought up in a poor home, having been kidnapped from the house of her rich father. He, having traced her to her husband's home, brings her back to him, and celebrates her marriage once again in a fitting manner.

In the concluding scene, when the husband is going through his period of penitence and humiliation, as is fit in a play which has a moral, a sudden disturbance arose among the audience. So long as Manorama appeared obscured in her position of drudgery Gopinath showed no sign of perturbation; but when after the wedding ceremony she came out dressed in her red bridal robe, and took her veil off, when with majestic pride of her overwhelming beauty she turned her face towards the audience and, slightly bending her neck, shot a fiery glance of exultation at Gopinath, applause broke out in wave after wave, and the enthusiasm of the spectators became unbounded.

Suddenly Gopinath cried out in a thick voice, 'Giribala,' and like a madman tried to rush upon the stage. The audience shouted, 'Turn him out,' the police came to drag him away, and he struggled and screamed, 'I will kill her,' while the curtain dropped.

THE LOST JEWELS

My boat was moored beside an old bathing ghat of the river, almost in ruins. The sun had set.

On the roof of the boat the boatmen were at their evening prayer. Against the bright background of the western sky their silent worship stood out like a picture. The waning light was reflected on the still surface of river in every delicate shade of colour from gold to steel-blue.

A huge house with broken windows, tumbledown verandas, and all the appearance of old age was in front of me. I sat alone on the steps of the ghat, which were cracked by the far-reaching roots of a banyan tree. A feeling of sadness began to come over me, when suddenly I was startled to hear a voice asking: 'Sir, where have you come from?'

I looked up, and saw a man who seemed half-starved and out of fortune. His face had a dilapidated look such as is common among my countrymen who take up service away from home. His dirty coat of Assam silk was greasy and open at the front. He appeared to be just returning from his day's work, and to be taking a walk by the side of the river at a time when he should have been eating his evening meal.

The new-comer sat beside me on the steps. I said in answer to his question: 'I come from Ranchi.'

'What occupation?'

'I am a merchant.'

'What sort?'

'A dealer in cocoons and timber.'

'What name?'

After a moment's hesitation I gave a name, but it was not my own.

Still the stranger's curiosity was not satisfied. Again he questioned me: 'What have you come here for?' I replied: 'For a change of air.'

My cross-examiner seemed a little astonished. He said: 'Well, sir, I have been enjoying the air of this place for nearly six years, and with it I have taken a daily average of fifteen grains of quinine, but I have not noticed that I have benefited much.'

I replied: 'Still, you must acknowledge that, after Ranchi, I shall find the air of this place sufficient of a change.'

'Yes, indeed,' said he. 'More than you bargain for. But where will you stay here?'

Pointing to the tumble-down house above the ghat, I said: 'There.'

I think my friend had a suspicion that I had come in search of hidden treasure. However, he did not pursue the subject. He only began to describe to me what had happened in this ruined building some fifteen years before.

I found that he was the schoolmaster of the place. From beneath an enormous bald head, his two eyes shone out from their sockets with an unnatural brightness in a face that was thin with hunger and illness.

The boatmen, having finished their evening prayer, turned their attention to their cooking. As the last light of the day faded, the dark and empty house stood silent and ghostly above the deserted ghat.

The schoolmaster said: 'Nearly ten years ago, when I came to this place, Bhusan Saha used to live in this house. He was the heir to the large property and business of his uncle Durga Saha, who was childless.

'But he was modern. He had been educated, and not only spoke faultless English, but actually entered sahibs' offices with his shoes on. In addition to that he grew a beard; thus he had not the least chance of bettering himself so far as the sahibs were concerned. You had only to look at him to see that he was a modernised Bengali.

'In his own home, too, he had another drawback. His wife was beautiful. With his college education on the one hand, and on the other his beautiful wife, what chance was there of his preserving our good old traditions in his home? In fact, when he was ill, he actually called in the assistant surgeon. And his style of food, dress, and his wife's jewels were all on the same extravagant scale.

'Sir, you are certainly a married man, so that it is hardly necessary to tell you that the ordinary female is fond of sour green mangoes, hot chillies, and a stern husband. A man need not necessarily be ugly or poor to be cheated of his wife's love; but he is sure to lose it if he is too gentle.

'If you ask me why this is so, I have much to say on this subject, for I have thought a good deal about it. A deer chooses a hardwood tree on which to sharpen its horns, and would get no pleasure in rubbing its horns against the soft stem of a plantain tree. From the very moment that man and woman became separate sexes, woman has been exercising all her faculties in trying by various devices to fascinate and bring man under her control. The wife of a man who is, of his own accord, submissive is altogether out of employment. All those weapons which she has inherited from her grandmothers of untold centuries are useless in her hands: the force of her tears, the fire of her anger, and the snare of her glances lie idle.

'Under the spell of modern civilisation man has lost the God-given power of his barbaric nature, and this has loosened the conjugal ties. The unfortunate Bhusan had been turned out of the machine of modern civilisation an absolutely faultless man. He was therefore neither successful in business nor in his own home.

'Mani was Bhusan's wife. She used to get her caresses without asking, her Dacca muslin saris without tears, and her bangles without being able to pride herself on a victory. In this way her woman's nature became atrophied, and with it her love for her husband. She simply accepted things without giving anything in return. Her harmless and foolish husband used to imagine that to give is the way to get. The fact was just the contrary.

'The result of this was that Mani looked upon her husband as a mere machine for turning out her Dacca muslins and her bangles, so perfect a machine, indeed, that never for a single day did she need to oil its wheels.

'Though Bhusan's birthplace was Phulbere, here was his place of business, where, for the sake of his work, he spent most of his time. At his Phulbere house he had no mother, but had plenty of aunts and uncles and other relatives, from which distraction he brought away his wife to this house and kept her to himself alone. But there is this difference between a wife and one's other possessions, that by keeping her to oneself one may lose her beyond recovery.

'Bhusan's wife did not talk very much, nor did she mix much with her neighbours. To feed Brahmans in obedience to a sacred vow, or to give a few pice to a religious mendicant, was not her way. In her hands nothing was ever lost; whatever she got she saved up most carefully, with the one exception of the memory of her husband's caresses. The extraordinary thing was that she did not seem to lose the least atom of her youthful beauty. People said that whatever her age was, she never looked older than sixteen. I suppose youth is best preserved with the aid of a heart that is an ice-box.

'But as far as work was concerned Mani was very efficient. She never kept more servants than were absolutely necessary. She thought that to pay wages to any one to do work which she herself could do was like playing the pickpocket with her own money.

'Not being anxious about any one, never being distracted by love, always working and saving, she was never sick nor sorry.

'For the majority of husbands this is quite sufficient, not only sufficient, but fortunate. For the loving wife is a wife who makes it difficult for her husband to forget her, and the fatigue of perpetual remembrance wears out life's bloom. It is only when a man has lumbago that he becomes conscious of his waist. And lumbago in domestic affairs is to be made conscious, by the constant imposition of love, that you have such a thing as a wife. Excessive devotion to her husband may be a merit for the wife but not comfortable for the husband, that is my candid opinion.

'I hope I am not tiring you, sir? I live alone, you see; I am banished from the company of my wife, and there are many important social questions which I have leisure to think about, but cannot discuss with my pupils. In course of conversation you will see how deeply I have thought of them.'

Just as he was speaking, some jackals began to howl from a neighbouring thicket. The schoolmaster stopped for a moment the torrent of his talk. When the sound had ceased, and the earth and the water relapsed into a deeper silence, he opened his glowing eyes wide in the darkness of the night, and resumed the thread of his story.

'Suddenly a tangle occurred in Bhusan's complicated business. What exactly happened it is not possible for a layman like myself either to understand or to explain. Suffice it to say that, for some sudden reason, he found it difficult to get credit in the market. If only he could, by hook or by crook, raise a lakh and a half of rupees, and only for a few days rapidly flash it before the market, then his credit would be restored, and he would be able to sail fair again.

'But the money did not come easily. If the rumour got about that he was borrowing in the market where he was known, then he feared that his business would suffer even more seriously. So he began to cast about to see whether he could not raise a loan from some stranger. But, in that case, he would be bound to give some satisfactory security.

'The best security of all is jewelry, for that saves the signing of all sorts of complicated documents. It not only saves time but is a simple process.

'So Bhusan went to his wife. But unfortunately he was not able to face his wife as easily as most men are. His love for his wife was of that kind which has to tread very carefully, and cannot speak out plainly what is in the mind; it is like the attraction of the sun for the earth, which is strong, yet which leaves immense space between them.

'Still, even the hero of a high-class romance does sometimes, when hard pressed, have to mention to his beloved such things as mortgage deeds and promissory notes. But the words stick, and the tune does not seem right, and the shrinking of reluctance makes itself felt. The unfortunate Bhusan was totally powerless to say: "Look here, I am in need of money; bring out your jewels."

'He did broach the subject to his wife at last, but with such extreme delicacy that it only excited her opposition without bending it to his own purpose. When Mani set her face hard, and said nothing, he was deeply hurt, yet he was incapable of returning the hurt back to her. The reason was that he had not even a trace of that barbarity which is the gift of the male. If any one had upbraided him for this, then most probably he would have expressed some such subtle sentiment as the following: "If my wife, of her own free choice, is unwilling to trust me with her jewelry, then I have no right to take them from her by force."

'Has God given to man such forcefulness only for him to spend his time in delicate measurement of fine-spun ideals?

'However this may be, Bhusan, being too proud to touch his wife's jewels, went to Calcutta to try some other way of raising the money.

'As a general rule in this world, the wife knows the husband far better than the husband ever knows the wife; but extremely modern men in their subtlety of nature are altogether beyond the range of those unsophisticated instincts which womankind has acquired through ages. These men are a new race, and have become as mysterious as women themselves. Ordinary men can be divided roughly into three main classes; some of them are barbarians, some are fools, and some are blind; but these modern men do not fit into any of them.

'So Mani called her counsellor for consultation. Some cousin of hers was engaged as assistant steward on Bhusan's estate. He was not the kind of man to profit himself by dint of hard work, but by help of his position in the family he was able to save his salary, and even a little more.

'Mani called him and told him what had happened. She ended up by asking him: "Now what is your advice?"

'He shook his head wisely and said: "I don't like the look of things at all." The fact is that wise men never like the look of things. Then he added: "Babu will never be able to raise the money, and in the end he will have to fall back upon that jewelry of yours."

'From what she knew of humanity she thought that this was not only possible but likely. Her anxiety became keener than ever. She had no child to love, and though she had a husband she was almost unable to realise his very existence. So her blood froze at the very thought that her only object of love, the wealth which like a child had grown from year to year, was to be in a moment thrown into the bottomless abyss of trade. She gasped: "What, then, is to be done?"

'Modhu said: "Why not take your jewels and go to your father's house?" In his heart of hearts he entertained the hope that a portion, and possibly the larger portion, of that jewelry would fall to his lot.

'Mani at once agreed. It was a rainy night towards the end of summer. At this very ghat a boat was moored. Mani, wrapped from head to foot in a thick shawl, stepped into the boat. The frogs croaked in the thick darkness of the cloudy dawn. Modhu, waking up from sleep, roused himself from the boat, and said: "Give me the box of jewels."

'Mani replied: "Not now, afterwards. Now let us start."

'The boat started, and floated swiftly down the current. Mani had spent the whole night in covering every part of her body with her ornaments. She was afraid that if she put her jewels into a box they might be snatched away from her hands. But if she wore them on her person, then no one could take them away without murdering her. Mani did not understand Bhusan, it is true; but there was no doubt about her understanding of Modhu.

'Modhu had written a letter to the chief steward to the effect that he had started to take his mistress to her father's house. The steward was an ancient retainer of Bhusan's father. He was furiously angry, and wrote a lengthy epistle, full of misspellings, to his master. Although the letter was weak in its grammar, yet it was forcible in its language, and clearly expressed the writer's disapproval of giving too much indulgence to womankind. Bhusan on receiving it understood what was the motive of Mani's secret departure. What hurt him most was the fact that, in spite of his having given way to the unwillingness of his wife to part with her jewels in this time of his desperate straits, his wife should still suspect him.

'When he ought to have been angry, Bhusan was only distressed. Man is the rod of God's justice, to him has been entrusted the thunderbolt of the divine wrath, and if at wrong done to himself or another it does not at once break out into fury, then it is a shame. God has so arranged it that man, for the most trifling reason, will burst forth in anger like a forest fire, and woman will burst into tears like a rain-cloud for no reason at all. But the cycle seems to have changed, and this appears no longer to hold good.

'The husband bent his head, and said to himself: "Well, if this is your judgment, let it be so. I will simply do my own duty." Bhusan, who ought to have been born five or six centuries hence, when the world will be moved by psychic forces, was unfortunate enough not only to be born in the nineteenth century, but also to marry a woman who belonged to that primitive age which persists through all time. He did not write a word on the subject to his wife, and determined in his mind that he would never mention it to her again. What an awful penalty!

'Ten or twelve days later, having secured the necessary loan, Bhusan returned to his home. He imagined that Mani, after completing her mission, had by this time come back from her father's house. And so he approached the door of the inner apartments, wondering whether his wife would show any signs of shame or penitence for the undeserved suspicion with which she had treated him.

'He found that the door was shut. Breaking the lock, he entered the room, and saw that it was empty.

'It seemed to him that the world was a huge cage from which the bird of love had flown away, leaving behind it all the decorations of the blood-red rubies of our hearts, and the pearl pendants of our tear-drops.

'At first Bhusan did not trouble about his wife's absence. He thought that if she wanted to come back she would do so. His old Brahman steward, however, came to him, and said: "What good will come of taking no notice of it? You ought to get some news of the mistress." Acting on this suggestion, messengers were sent to Mani's father's house. The news was brought that up to that time neither Mani nor Modhu had turned up there.

'Then a search began in every direction. Men went along both banks of the river making inquiries. The police were given a description of Modhu, but all in vain. They were unable to find out what boat they had taken, what boatman they had hired, or by what way they had gone.

'One evening, when all hope had been abandoned of ever finding his wife, Bhusan entered his deserted bedroom. It was the festival of Krishna's birth, and it had been raining incessantly from early morning. In celebration of the festival there was a fair going on in the village, and in a temporary building a theatrical performance was being given. The sound of distant singing could be heard mingling with the sound of pouring rain. Bhusan was sitting alone in the darkness at the window there which hangs loose upon its hinges. He took no notice of the damp wind, the spray of the rain, and the sound of the singing. On the wall of the room were hanging a couple of pictures of the goddesses Lakshmi and Saraswati, painted at the Art Studio; on the clothes-rack a towel, and a bodice, and a pair of saris were laid out ready for use. On a table in one corner of the room there was a box containing betel leaves prepared by Mani's own hand, but now quite dry and uneatable. In a cupboard with a glass door all sorts of things were arranged with evident care, her china dolls of childhood's days, scent bottles, decanters of coloured glass, a sumptuous pack of cards, large brightly polished shells, and even empty soapboxes. In a niche there was a favourite little lamp with its round globe. Mani had been in the habit of lighting it with her own hands every evening. One who goes away, leaving everything empty, leaves the imprint of his living heart even on lifeless objects. Come, Mani, come back again, light your lamp, fill your room with light once more, and, standing before your mirror, put on your sari which has been prepared with such care. See, all your things are waiting for you. No one will claim anything more from you, but only ask you to give a living unity once more to these scattered and lifeless things, by the mere presence of your imperishable youth and unfading beauty. Alas, the inarticulate cry of these mute and lifeless objects has made this room into a realm of things that have lost their world.

'In the dead of night, when the heavy rain had ceased, and the songs of the village opera troupe had become silent, Bhusan was sitting in the same position as before. Outside the window there was such an impenetrable darkness that it seemed to him as if the very gates of oblivion were before him reaching to the sky, as if he had only to cry out to be able to recover sight of those things which seemed to have been lost forever.

'Just as he was thinking thus, a jingling sound as of ornaments was heard. It seemed to be advancing up the steps of the ghat. The water of the river and the darkness of the night were indistinguishable. Thrilling with excitement, Bhusan tried to pierce and push through the darkness with his eager eyes, till they ached, but he could see nothing. The more anxious he was to see, the denser the darkness became, and the more shadowy the outer world. Nature, seeing an intruder at the door of her hall of death, seemed suddenly to have drawn a still thicker curtain of darkness.

'The sound reached the top step of the bathing ghat, and now began to come towards the house. It stopped in front of the door, which had been locked by the porter before he went to the fair. Then upon that closed door there fell a rain of jingling blows, as if with some ornaments. Bhusan was not able to sit still another moment, but, making his way through the unlighted rooms and down the dark staircase, he stood before the closed door. It was padlocked from the outside, so he began to shake it with all his might. The force with which he shook the door and the sound which he made woke him suddenly. He found he had been asleep, and in his sleep he had made his way down to the door of the house. His whole body was wet with sweat, his hands and feets were icy cold, and his heart was fluttering like a lamp just about to go out. His dream being broken, he realised that there was no sound outside except the pattering of the rain which had commenced again.

'Although the whole thing was a dream, Bhusan felt as if for some very small obstacle he had been cheated of the wonderful realisation of his impossible hope. The incessant patter of the rain seemed to say to him: "This awakening is a dream. This world is vain."

'The festival was continued on the following day, and the doorkeeper again had leave. Bhusan gave orders that the hall-door was to be left open all night, but the porter objected that there were all sorts of suspicious characters about who had come from other places to the fair, and that it would not be safe to leave the door open. But Bhusan would not listen, whereupon the porter said that he would himself stay on guard. But Bhusan refused to allow him to remain. The porter was puzzled, but did not press the point.

'That night, having extinguished the light, Bhusan took his seat at the open window of his bedroom as before. The sky was dark with rain-clouds, and there was a silence as of something indefinite and impending. The monotonous croaking of the frogs and the sound of the distant songs were not able to break that silence, but only seemed to add an incongruity to it.

'Late at night the frogs and the crickets and the boys of the opera party became silent, and a still deeper darkness fell upon the night. It seemed that now the time had come.

'Just as on the night before, a clattering and jingling sound came from the ghat by the river. But this time Bhusan did not look in that direction, lest, by his over-anxiety and restlessness, his power of sight and hearing would become overwhelmed. He made a supreme effort to control himself, and sat still.

'The sound of the ornaments gradually advanced from the ghat, and entered the open door. Then it came winding up the spiral staircase which led to the inner apartments. It became difficult for Bhusan to control himself, his heart began to thump wildly, and his throat was choking with suppressed excitement. Having reached the head of the spiral stairs, the sound came slowly along the veranda towards the door of the room, where it stopped just outside with a clanking sound. It was now only just on the other side of the threshold.

'Bhusan could contain himself no longer, and his pent-up excitement burst forth in one wild cry of "Mani," and he sprang up from his chair with lightning rapidity. Thus startled out of his sleep, he found that the very window-panes were rattling with the vibration of his cry. And outside he could hear the croaking of the frogs and patter of rain. 'Bhusan struck his forehead in despair.

'Next day the fair broke up, and the stall-keepers and the players' party went away. Bhusan gave orders that that night no one should sleep in the house except himself. The servants came to the conclusion that their master was going to practise some mystic rites. All that day Bhusan fasted.

'In the evening, he took his seat at the window of that empty house. That day there were breaks in the clouds, showing the stars twinkling through-the rain-washed air. The moon was late in rising, and, as the fair was over, there was not a single boat on the flooded river. The villagers, tired out by two nights' dissipation, were sound asleep.

'Bhusan, sitting with his head resting on the back of his chair, was gazing up at the stars. He was thinking of the time when he was only nineteen years old, and was reading in Calcutta; how in the evening he used to lie in College Square, with his hands behind his head, gazing up at those eternal stars, and thinking of the sweet face of Mani in his father-in-law's house. The very separation from her was like an instrument whose tense-drawn strings those stars used to touch and waken into song.

'As he watched them, the stars one by one disappeared. From the sky above, and from the earth beneath, screens of darkness met like tired eyelids upon weary eyes. To-night Bhusan's mind was full of peace. He felt certain that the moment had come when his heart's desire would be fulfilled, and that Death would reveal his mysteries to his devotee.

'The sound came from the river ghat just as on the previous nights and advanced up the steps. Bhusan closed his eyes, and sat in deep meditation. The sound reached the empty hall. It came winding up the spiral stairs. Then it crossed the long veranda, and paused for a long while at the bedroom door.

'Bhusan's heart beat fast; his whole body trembled. But this time he did not open his eyes. The sound crossed the threshold. It entered the room. Then it went slowly round the room, stopping before the rack where the clothes were hanging, the niche with its little lamp, the table where the dried betel leaves were lying, the almirah with its various knick-knacks, and, last of all, it came and stood close to Bhusan himself.

'Bhusan opened his eyes. He saw by the faint light of the crescent moon that there was a skeleton standing right in front of his chair. It had rings on all its fingers, bracelets on its wrists and armlets on its arms, necklaces on its neck, and a golden tiara on its head, in fact its whole body glittered and sparkled with gold and diamonds. The ornaments hung loosely on the limbs, but did not fall off. Most dreadful of all was the fact that the two eyes which shone out from the bony face were living, two dark moist eyeballs looking out with a fixed and steady stare from between the long thick eyelashes. As he looked his blood froze in his veins. He tried hard to close his eyes but could not; they remained open, staring like those of a dead man.

'Then the skeleton, fixing its gaze upon the face of the motionless Bhusan, silently beckoned with its outstretched hand, the diamond rings on its bony fingers glittering in the pale moonlight.

'Bhusan stood up, as one who had lost his senses, and followed the skeleton, which left the room, its bones and ornaments rattling with a hollow sound. The skeleton crossed the veranda and, winding down the pitch-dark spiral staircase, reached the bottom of the stairs. Crossing the lower veranda, they entered the empty lampless hall and, passing through it, came out on to the brick-paved path of the garden. The bricks crunched under the tread of the bony feet. The faint moonlight struggled through the thick network of branches, and the path was difficult to discern. Making their way through the flitting fireflies, which haunted the dark shadowy path, they reached the river ghat.

'By those very steps, up which the sound had come, the bejewelled skeleton went down step by step, with a stiff gait and hard sound. On the swift current of the river, flooded by the heavy rain, a faint streak of moonlight was visible.

'The skeleton descended to the river, and Bhusan, following it, placed one foot in the water. The moment he touched the water he woke with a start. His guide was no longer to be seen. Only the trees on the opposite bank of the river were standing still and silent, and overhead the half moon was staring as if astonished. Starting from head to foot, Bhusan slipped and fell headlong into the river. Although he knew how to swim, he was powerless to do so, for his limbs were not under his control. From the midst of dreams he had stepped, for a moment only, into the borderland of waking life, the next moment to be plunged into eternal sleep.'

Having finished his story, the schoolmaster was silent for a little. Suddenly, the moment he stopped, I realised that except for him the whole world had become silent and still. For a long time I also remained speechless, and in the darkness he was unable to see from my face what was its expression.

At last he asked me: 'Don't you believe this story?'

I asked: 'Do you?'

He said: 'No; and I can give you one or two reasons why. In the first place, Dame Nature does not write novels, she has enough to do without -'

I interrupted him and said: 'And, in the second place, my name happens to be Bhusan Saha.'

The schoolmaster, without the least sign of discomfiture, said: 'I guessed as much. And what was your wife's name?'

I answered: 'Nitya Kali.'

EMANCIPATION

'Theft from the king's treasury!' The cry ran through the town. The thief must be found, or there will be trouble for the officer of the guards.

Vajrasen, a stranger from a foreign port, came to sell horses in the town, and, robbed by a band of robbers of all his earnings, was lying in a ruined temple outside the walls. They charged him with the theft, chained him, and led him through the streets to the prison.

Proud Shyama, of a perilous charm, sat in her balcony idly watching the passing crowd. Suddenly she shuddered, and cried to her attendant: 'Alas, who is that godlike young man with a noble face, led in chains like a common thief? Ask the officer in my name to bring him in before me.'

The chief of the guards came with the prisoner, and said to Shyama: 'Your favour is untimely, my lady; I must hasten to do the king's bidding.' Vajrasen quickly raised his head, and broke out: 'What caprice is this of yours, woman, to bring me in from the street to mock me with your cruel curiosity?'

'Mock you!' cried Shyama; 'I could gladly take your chains upon my limbs in exchange for my jewels.'

Then turning to the officer, she said: 'Take all the money I have, and set him free.'

He bowed, and said: 'It cannot be. A victim we must have to stay the king's wrath.'

'I ask only two days' respite for the prisoner,' urged Shyama. The officer smiled, and consented.

On the end of his second night in prison, Vajrasen said his prayers, and sat waiting for his last moment, when suddenly the door opened, and the woman appeared with a lamp in her hand, and at her signal the guard unchained the prisoner.

'You have come to me with that lamp, merciful woman,' said he, 'like the dawn with her morning star after a night of delirious fever.'

'Merciful indeed,' Shyama cried, and broke out in wild laughter, till tears came with a burst, and she sobbed, and said: 'There is no stone brick in this prison-tower harder than this woman's heart.' And clutching the prisoner's hand she dragged him out of the gates.

On the Varuna's bank the sun rose. A boat was waiting at the landing. 'Come to the boat with me, stranger youth,' Shyama said. 'Only know that I have cut all bonds, and I drift in the same boat with you.'

Swiftly the boat glided on. Merrily sang the birds. 'Tell me, my love,' asked Vajrasen, 'what untold wealth did you spend to buy my freedom?'

'Hush, not now,' said Shyama.

Morning wore on to noon. Village women had gone back home with their clothes dripping from their bath, and pitchers filled with water. Marketing was over. The village path glared in the sun all lonely.

In the warm gusts of the noontide wind Shyama's veil dropped from her face. Vajrasen murmured in her ears: 'You freed me from a bond that was brief to bind me in a bond everlasting. Let me know how it was done.' The woman drew her veil over her face, and said: 'Not now, my beloved.'

The day waned, and it darkened. The breeze died away. The crescent moon glimmered feebly at the edge of the steel-black water.

Shyama sat in the dark, resting her head on the youth's shoulder. Her hair fell loose on his arms.

'What I did for you was hard, beloved,' she said in a faint whisper,'but it is harder to tell you. I shall tell it in a few words. It was the love-sick boy Uttiya who took your place, charging himself with the theft, and making me a present of his life. My greatest sin has been committed for the love of you, my best beloved.'

While she spoke the crescent moon had set. The stillness of the forest was heavy with the sleep of countless birds.

Slowly the youth's arm slipped from the woman's waist. Silence round them became hard and cold as stone.

Suddenly the woman fell at his feet, and clung to his knee crying: 'Forgive me, my love. Leave it to my God to punish me for my sin.'

Snatching his feet away, Vajrasen hoarsely cried: 'That my life should be bought by the price of a sin! That every breath of mine should be accursed!'

He stood up, and leapt from the boat on the bank, and entered the forest. He walked on and on till the path closed and the dense trees, tangled with creepers, stopped him with fantastic gestures.

Tired, he sat on the ground. But who was it that followed him in silence, the long dark way, and stood at his back like a phantom?

'Will you not leave me?' shouted Vajrasen.

In a moment the woman fell upon him with an impetuous flood of caresses; with her tumbling hair and trailing robes, with her showering kisses and panting breath she covered him all over.

In a voice choked with pent-up tears, she said: 'No, no; I shall never leave you. I have sinned for you. Strike me, if you will; kill me with your own hands.'

The still blackness of the forest shivered for a moment; a horror ran through the twisting roots of trees underground. A groan and a smothered breath rose through the night, and a body fell down upon the withered leaves.

The morning sun flashed on the far-away spire of the temple when Vajrasen came out of the woods. He wandered in the hot sun the whole day by the river on the sandy waste, and never rested for a moment.

In the evening he went back aimlessly to the boat. There on the bed lay an anklet. He clutched it, and pressed it to his heart till it bruised him. He fell prone upon the blue mantle left lying in a heap in the corner, hid his face in its folds, and from its silken touch and evasive fragrance struggled to absorb into his being the memory of a dear living body.

The night shook with a tense and tingling silence. The moon disappeared behind the trees. Vajrasen stood up, and stretched out his arms towards the woods, and called: 'Come, my love, come.'

Suddenly a figure came out of the darkness, and stood on the brink of the water.

'Come, love, come.'

'I have come, my beloved. Your dear hands failed to kill me. It is my doom to live.'

Shyama came, and stood before the youth. He looked at her face, he moved a step to take her in his arms, then thrust her away with both hands, and cried: 'Why, oh why did you come back?'

He shut his eyes, turning his face, and said: 'Go, go; leave me.'

For a minute the woman stood silent before she knelt at his feet and bowed low. Then she rose, and went up the river-bank, and vanished in the vague of the woods like a dream merging into sleep; and Vajrasen, with aching heart, sat silent in the boat.

A Biography

Rabindranath Tagore (1861-1941) is an Indian poet, playwright, novelist, composer, painter and a national icon of his country. His profuse literary production ranges from collections of poems such as *Manasi* (1890), *Gitanjali* (1910) and Patraput (1936) to drama such as *Visarjan* (1890), *Raja* (1910), *Muktadhara* (1922) and *Chandalika* (1938) and even numerous musical compositions and songs. In addition, Tagore's publications include a number of novels and several volumes of short stories including his widely appreciated *Gora* (1910) along with *Chaturanga* (1916) and *Ghare-Baire* (1916). The latter is one of his many works that were adapted to cinema.

Born in Calcutta, India, to a well-off family, Rabindranath Tagore was raised and educated mainly by servants. His father Devendranath Tagore is a saint and a religious leader of the Adi Dham faith and the Brahmo sect founded by the family's patriarchs. Young Rabindranath Tagore's home was animated by discussions of literary publications, arts, theatrical performances and classical music where most of his 14 siblings were much interested in arts, poetry, music, philosophy and theatre, such as his older sister, Swarnakumari Devi, the renowned Indian novelist, poet and musician.

In addition to such a supportive environment for artistic appreciation and creativity, Tagore's father made him discover language, literature, history and poetry, taking him for long journeys around the country. In 1873, they both left home for the hill station at Dalhousie. Named after the British Governor-General Lord Dalhousie who used to visit it during his summer holidays, the station is surrounded by captivating green hills and heaven-like vistas. During the months spent there, Tagore must have found in the station's assortments of Hindu art and temples, along with the European architecture of its summer residences, a magnificent blending of East and West.

Readers of Tagore's poetry, novels and short stories, such as "The Fruitseller from Kabul," to name but a sample, can surely detect in their imagery and emotional outlets the influence of Dalhousie's breath-taking sceneries and verdure. Tagore's journey with his father was mainly meant to be a necessary stage towards intellectual and moral maturity and individuation. The lessons that the father transmitted to the son in such an inspirational spot were not only meant to be informational lessons but also spiritual ones. Indeed, being a very respected spiritual figure who wished to hand on the torch to younger disciples, Tagore's father inculcated in him mystical yearnings for spiritual knowledge and existential meaning.

It is, however, noteworthy that despite his conspicuous lust for knowledge, Tagore hated the "yoke" of formal education and thought that classroom teaching could only muffle young people's innate and instinctive thirst for discovery and adventure. The two long journeys that he had with his father only reinforced this attitude as they helped nourish his love for nature and the divine. Helped by his father, his brother Hemendranath and the house servants, Tagore studied language, literature, mathematics, geography and history and practiced different sports at home and in the family's manor. When his father sent him to London to study law in 1878, he quickly left University College London and chose to study language, literature and music by himself. Two years later, he travelled back to India without getting the formal degree he was sent for.

Tagore expressed in many an occasion his belief that teaching should arouse curiosity rather than be informative and he strove to put his ideas into practice particularly by founding the Visva-Bharati school, which has now become the Visva-Bharati University, where he established the "brahmacharya" educational system. The main characteristic of Tagore's educational conception was to have teachers incite their students to discover and learn through employing intellectual and spiritual motivational strategies.

As for his writings, Tagore was a genuine prodigy who started weaving his earliest verses by the age of eight in the family's Calcutta residence. A few years later, he pseudonymously published his first collection of poems which was an astounding success to the point that local critics thought the compilation to belong to the 17th-century poet Bhanusimha. He soon shifted to writing short stories and plays to achieve considerable fame in the region. While all his writings were in his native Bengali language, he eventually decided to address Western readers by translating some of his own works into English.

The English versions of his poetic works such as *Manasi* (1890), *Gitimalya* (1914) and mainly what is today considered in the West as his magnum opus, *Gitanjali* (1910), quickly gained ground among Western literary circles. Such works were read, reviewed and prefaced by leading literary figures of the time like William Butler Yeats and Ezra Pound. Tagore soon became an oriental icon who stands for India's literary, spiritual and cultural heritage. In 1913, the relatively small part of his works discovered by the West earned him the Nobel Prize in Literature. In 1915, he was also knighted by the British Crown for his literary achievements.

Once famous in the West, Tagore toured Britain and the United States and lectured in many other European and non-European countries to meet and interact with important celebrities around the world including the celebrated German-born physicist Albert Einstein, Thomas Mann, George Bernard Shaw and H.G. Wells, among many others.

Politically, while Tagore's commitment manifested in his harsh criticism of nationalist extremism and in his avant-garde and reformatory positions at home, he denounced imperialism and advocated universalism and internationalism in the world. In India, he was known for his rejection of the culture of victimhood and for inciting his countrymen to have the courage of assuming the responsibilities of their misfortunes. He saw that salvation could only be realized through education and self-help. In addition to that, Tagore was also socially active in his homeland, supporting students and the poor. As for foreign affairs, Tagore denounced British colonialism and even renounced the honor previously granted by the British Crown in protest against the 1919 Jallianwala Bagh massacre.

Such political views were explicitly expressed in some of Tagore's writings and musical compositions, two of which were chosen by India and Bangladesh as national anthems. His friend Mahatma Gandhi, the celebrated leader of the Indian nationalist movement, expressed his appreciation of these compositions and was said to favor the "Ekla Chalo Re" hymn.

Towards the twilight of his career, Tagore developed new interests, mainly in arts, paintings and sciences. This is mainly expressed in stories like *Se* (1937) and *Tin Sangi* (1940) as well as in his collection of essays entitled *Visva-Parichay* (1937) which represents a literary man's exploration of the fields of astronomy, physics and biology. He even took up drawing and painting at a late age and organized exhibitions of his works in Paris and other cities.

Towards the end of the 1930s, old Rabindranath Tagore's health started to deteriorate until he died on August 7th, 1941, leaving a gigantic oeuvre of numerous volumes of fine poetry, hundreds of texts, short stories, novels, plays, paintings, doodles, more than two thousand songs, two autobiographies and numerous travelogues, essays and lectures.

Tagore's life experience had taught him that divisions between human beings are nothing but an unpleasant mirage. Generally, his oeuvre invites and incites its readers to the exploration of the Other, the exploration of the Self. The following extract from his masterpiece *Gitanjali* may serve as a perfect illustration of Tagore's philosophical vision:

The time that my journey takes is long and the way of it long.
I came out on the chariot of the first gleam of light, and pursued my voyage through the wildernesses of worlds leaving my track on many a star and planet.
It is the most distant course that comes nearest to thyself, and that training is the most intricate which leads to the utter simplicity of a tune.
The traveller has to knock at every alien door to come to his own, and one has to wander through all the outer worlds to reach the innermost shrine at the end.
My eyes strayed far and wide before I shut them and said 'Here art thou!'
The question and the cry 'Oh, where?' melt into tears of a thousand streams and deluge the world with the flood of the assurance 'I am!' (Song XII)